I0672033

The Haunting Lessons

How to Survive and Thrive

When Armageddon Strikes

Book One of the Ghosts & Demons Series

Holly Pop and Robert Chazz Chute

Published by Ex Parte Press

First Edition: December 2014

Print Edition: January 2015

ISBN 978-1-927607-32-9

Media and rights inquiries should be directed to

expartepress@gmail.com.

*Dedicated to our readers*

*because we are*

*dedicated to our readers.*


*Special thanks for editorial assistance to Marissa*
*"Mama" Pop, Brian Wright, Russ Sawatsky and Dr.*
*Janice Kurita.*

**To find out when the next book in this series will**
**be released,**
**sign up for the update letter at AllThatChazz.com.**

*We learn words by rote, but not their meaning; that must be paid for with our life-blood, and printed in the subtle fibres of our nerves.*
*George Eliot, 1819 - 1880*
*The Lifted Veil*

**W**hen the nearly departed become the dearly departed, I'm the girl who takes them on their last ride. When strange men try to pick me up in the organic food aisle and ask me what I do, I tell them I'm a bodyguard. I tell them I train Rottweilers to castrate escaped felons. If I like the look of the guy and if he seems really nice and I'm trying to impress, I'll say I'm in the health services field. When I come clean on the first date and confess that I drive the dead, they usually want to skip dessert and there's no second date.

"I'll call you," they say.

"Sure. It was nice to meet you."

So much for trying to be a Normie. If they can't handle the fact that I drive a hearse occasionally, they really aren't up to the whole demon hunter thing. Normies don't pay attention to the concept of entropy. Normies don't see what's coming. Normies laugh more. I laugh a lot, too, but it's often the bitter, ironic kind. The crazy thing is, I used to be one of them — the Normies, I mean, not the demons.

Take a picture of me at seventeen: honor roll, year book editor, classical piano, popular small town girl, Senior Prom Princess. (Everybody likes the Princess more than the Queen, anyway. I'm the girl next-door, not the cheerleader headed off to fail in Hollywood.) I wasn't a cheerleader because Mom said I had to choose between cheerleading practice and martial arts. Cheerleaders and football players were the cool kids at Medicament Regional High School, but at age eleven, I told Mama that a black belt would set me apart on my college applications.

My plan was to get a degree in biology first and then apply to med school. I might have become a veterinarian if I could specialize in cats, dogs and horses.

Mama didn't want me to study martial arts. "What if they smoosh your nose?" she asked.

"If my nose gets broken," I told Mama, "maybe they can shave an inch off it and I could have a little button nose. This could work out well for me."

I was a Mama's girl because I didn't know where Daddy went. (Don't feel bad for me. That's good. It's one less person in my life to worry about. Later, I had to worry about him a lot.) Mama brought me up right. I was taught to say please and thank you and to nod and smile when older and better people talked down to me. I read a book a week. I was bound for big things but I was humble and sweet. Everybody said so. I know that much was real because my classmates wrote nice things in my yearbook like: *When you talked, you were always so funny in class,* and, *I wish I'd gotten to know you better,* and, *Brad & Tam 4Evah!*

Which brings us to Brad Evers. Brad had dimples so deep they were dents. He had such a great smile. That's what I noticed about him first and what I remember best. When I first spoke to Brad, we were only in seventh grade. A senior named Dave Cutcheon cut in front of me at a water fountain at school and I told him to wait his turn. The lug ignored me. Brad shoved the big guy back.

"You wanna *die,* little boy?" Cutcheon towered over my hero.

Brad looked him up and down, slow, and smiled. "You aren't really going to kill me. You aren't going to fight because you've got a game Friday night and you can't risk a suspension. The coach wouldn't like it. The team needs you, big guy."

Cutcheon grabbed Brad by the shirt and said, "Maybe I'll risk it."

"We both know you won't. Now show some respect. You're supposed to be a leader in the school. Won't do anything for your rep to be pushing around little kids."

"If your brother wasn't on the team, man — "

"Yeah, yeah," Brad said. "This was over a minute ago and we're all about to be late for class."

Cutcheon walked away.

That was Brad *in seventh grade.* We laughed together. He beamed that thousand watt smile at me. Then he galumphed down the hallway, clicking his tongue to mimic the sound of a galloping horse. Just as he disappeared around the corner he whinnied and called down the hall to me, "Who was that masked man? Hi, ho, Silver!

Away!"

He wasn't *my* Brad, yet, but I think I knew he would belong to me, even then.

That day I resolved to work harder every day after school to get my black belt. I decided I'd stay in Medicament, Iowa forever and I'd work at the little hospital I was born in. Each night, I'd come home to Brad's family farm and we'd have horses and cats and dogs and a couple of kids and we'd bring them up right, too.

There were a couple of flaws in my plan. Mama wouldn't let me date for two more years after what I came to think of as the Water Fountain Incident. I kept busy and getting that black belt was harder than I'd thought it would be. Reading books is much easier than sweating through endless drills. One of the things that kept me going was the thought that one day, with all my academic and physical training, I'd be worthy of the life I planned.

Mama was originally from Texas. She wouldn't budge on letting me date boys. When I pestered her about dating, demanding to know why I was the last of my classmates to date, Mama's answer was, "I'm from Amarillo." She's a stubborn woman. She taught me lots of things, mostly patience.

Flash forward to ninth grade. Allison Mackenzie, the school's prettiest redhead, started hanging around Brad. It seemed every time I saw Brad, Allison walked beside him, touching his muscular arms and laughing long and hard in a high titter. Allison had a thousand watt smile, too, but her main advantage was her push up bra. Her boobs and her annoying laugh spawned my secret nickname for Allison: High Titter.

I was sure I was losing the boy of my dreams to High Titter, but I was a go-getter. I had to go get him. I walked up to Brad, turned to smile at Allison and said, "Would you please excuse us? I have to talk to Brad about something."

I don't remember what she said. I don't think I gave her a chance to talk at all. I smiled wider and said, "Please? It's personal."

High Titter stalked off and that left Brad looking at me with wide eyes. My cheeks flushed hot and pink — I'm a blusher. I couldn't handle his gaze at close range so I stared at his dimples and glanced at his tanned arm muscles. I came straight out with it, talking into his dimples. "Are you going with Allison?"

"Not really."

"What does that mean?"

"She's in all my classes."

"And?"

He leaned closer and I could smell peppermint on his breath. "Between you and me, she's a little annoying."

"I think all the guys want to be with her, don't you?"

"Maybe they do, but I was in a crowded classroom on the first day of school and I heard her talk before I saw her."

"Sorry to be mean, but I suspected she wasn't so smart," I said. I wasn't sorry. I was mean.

He sighed. "Yeah. What she had to say kind of ruined the view." When I stopped laughing, he asked me what I wanted to talk about that was so personal.

"You remember that day you got Dave Cutcheon out of my way at the water fountain?"

"Yep."

5

"I never really thanked you."

"No big thing. Dave is washing cars at his dad's dealership now. No NFL for him. No more rude 'roid rage."

"That's a shame. So he really could have beaten you to death that day and he wouldn't have lost anything, huh?"

We laughed and I wanted to laugh with him more. I wanted to laugh with Brad Evers forever, so I asked, "Will you go with me to the Halloween Dance?"

"Yes." He didn't hesitate. I loved that he didn't hesitate.

For my first kiss, I was dressed in my gi from Mr. Chang's School of Hapkido. I had earned my red belt by then. Brad was dressed as a zombie, fake blood and all, in his older brother's black suit. That's how we began, Brad and Tam, Tam and Brad. We ended that way, as well, too soon. (Then the relationship continued on, too long past death…but I'll get to that.)

From junior high through high school, I had the most handsome, most kind and most confident farm boy boyfriend in all of Medicament, Iowa and probably the world. City people think living in a small town is boring. They don't know the joys of taking your boyfriend out to the tall grass and making love under the sun and stars.

Flash forward to the summer after graduation from high school. I worked part-time at Mama's drugstore stocking shelves. That's where I was when the world as I knew it began to come crashing down. I was putting throat lozenges on shelves and pricing them when I missed the last phone call Brad Evers ever made.

Sheriff Birch got to him before the paramedics arrived. Brad was smart enough to call 911 before he tried to call me, but by then he'd already lost too much blood. Brad saw what was coming. A trail of blood led the Sheriff to the open front door of the Evers house. The front door stood open and splintered. Brad was on the floor by the phone.

Medicament is a small town. By the end of the day, half of Medicament, Iowa knew that Sheriff Birch found my farm boy boyfriend with a number two pencil still in his teeth. The hay baler's engine was still chugging and its metal teeth were still turning, splattered red and hungry for more.

Flash forward a few days to my first funeral, the first of hundreds. Maybe, someday, Brad's funeral will be the first of thousands.

Now take a picture of me at nineteen: dressed in black, one hand on a closed casket, a single red rose in one hand. Mama's pulling me away and I don't want to leave. As soon as I leave, they're going to put my farm boy boyfriend down in the cold dark with the worms and grubs.

Mama gave me a sedative but I didn't want to sleep. I wanted to walk. Mama told me to look forward not back. "I know you don't feel normal," she said, "but you're still you. Brad was a good boy, but you are still the girl you were before he came along."

I didn't feel the same. I had finally earned a black belt from Mr. Chang. I'd graduated at the top of my class. Mama insisted I still had a bright future to blot out the shadows of the past. But you can't forget or replace a boyfriend like Brad Evers that easily.

His was a regular small town tragedy. Farm accidents happen all over rural America and all over the world every year. But people won't admit to the fact that death isn't always the end. Some of the dead hang on. Sometimes, something holds the dead back from going wherever they're supposed to go. For Brad, that something was me. That's a terrible burden to put on someone you love. It's selfish. The deep love that anchored him to me too strongly was the only fault in Brad I can recall.

Days after the funeral, I walked the road by the Evers house outside of town, the long fence stood on my right. I wasn't Brad's widow. I was just the dead boy's girlfriend. People don't give the plans of girlfriends and boyfriends weight. The love of my life was dead and when I talked about what might have been, people just shook their heads and asked if they could do anything. No, of course not. Then they asked if I wanted some cake or tea or to talk to a counselor. No. No. And definitely not.

"People don't know what to say to you, that's all," Mama said. "Nobody knows what to say when a young person dies. Soon, they'll give up saying anything because no one wants to think about it." She patted my arm. "What you don't understand yet, what's really tough to acknowledge right now is, that boy wasn't the love of your life. He was just your first love."

I love Mama, but I couldn't bear her saying that. That's what led me out on that lonely road, back to Brad's family's farm. I stared at the Evers farmhouse and thought about Christmas Eve. That was the first night I'd snuck into the Evers' house. His parents were out.

Later, I think his Dad suspected us. Brad and I couldn't keep our hands off each other and we smiled more than is considered appropriate in rural Iowa. But Mr. Evers said nothing and never frowned at me. I was already looking forward to calling Mr. Evers my father-in-law.

As I stood on the road in my black dress, I looked at the farm. I realized I wouldn't step into the Evers' home again. I had thought Brad and I might own that old house someday. I turned away. I wept and I began the long walk home. The long fence guarded the tall grass on my left. I caught a glimpse of someone in my peripheral vision. I turned and gasped. Brad watched me from the field.

At first I thought he was a hallucination born of the sedative Mama had given me. Then I thought it must be a scarecrow or a cruel joke. As I got closer, I thought it was Brad in his zombie makeup from our first date at the Halloween dance. Except now my farm boy boyfriend with the dents for dimples did not have muscular arms. He had no arms at all.

# 2

Lesson 1: when you see your dead boyfriend standing in the tall grass with no arms, tell no one. The Normies do not take this sort of information well or lightly.

The denial will come first and you'll really want to believe Mama's right. It's grief. It was a trick of the light. It was a reaction to the drugs that the pharmaceutical company failed to list on the label: *May cause drowsiness, suicidal ideation and seeing zombie boyfriends. Objects in the drug-distorted mirror may be weirder than they appear.*

But zombie isn't the right word, is it? Ghost, wraith, specter…dead boyfriend who won't move on. It adds a whole new dimension to stalking.

Lesson 2: when they send you to the doctor, he won't necessarily be sympathetic. Dr. Wilson was one of those old school, country docs. He was old enough to have pronounced time of death on a hundred accidents out in farm country: dangerous equipment, chain saw follies, hunting accidents, drunk driving on gravelly country roads. Unless they've driven at high speeds with clouds of dust and dirt billowing from the rear wheels, people don't know — sometimes until it's too late — that a dirt road may as well be ice if you're flooring the accelerator.

"You think you're the first person to experience loss, girl?" Dr. Wilson asked.

"No," I said. "I know Brad's mom and dad and his older brother have suffered a terrible loss. They won't recover from it. But they don't see the person they've lost every time they look out the window."

Zombie Brad stood beneath my bedroom window every night. At first all I saw was his silhouette. I was too afraid to shine a flashlight beam down into the yard. I screamed for Mama, of course. All she saw was shadows cast by the branches of the oak tree. She held me as I cried and then the moon came out and Brad was no longer a silhouette. He was a zombie ghost amputee staring up, maybe at me, maybe at the full moon. And smiling his dimpled smile.

I felt his love like a cold hand over my heart. I wanted my farm boy boyfriend to go away. Wanting that was worst of all.

Mama still couldn't see him. That's when I really knew I wasn't a Normie, anymore.

Lesson 3: When the drugs don't work they'll try to send you to the local hospital. Don't go. There are more fresh dead people there standing around and looking for a sympathetic person who can see them.

I walked into the ER through automatic doors with Mama, cooperative and hopeful that somebody could help me. Dr. Wilson hadn't been the one to help me, but surely someone else had gone through what I had. It was a grief thing.

"Grief," Mama assured me, "is transient. You're going to get past this. It's just the shock, is all."

That made sense. I thought so, too. I would have held on to that idea longer, but a dead guy stood beside the admitting nurse. He was a middle-aged man, thick in the middle. He wore a hospital gown. He stood behind the nurse at the admitting desk and stared at her. I would have thought he was alive except he looked waxy. The dead don't really look pale. Waxy is the word. Then the waxy man's eyes met mine.

The nurse looked up at me from her desk, her mouth tight behind carelessly applied lipstick. "Name?"

When I didn't say anything, Mama answered for me. "Tamara Smythe."

"What's the problem, Tamara Smythe?"

I opened my mouth and I said, "I don't think this is just indigestion."

The nurse sat straight as if a live electrical wire was shoved up her spine. She sputtered. "Wh-what did you say?"

Hot tears streamed down my face. "It's not indigestion. Tums ain't gonna do it."

The nurse stood, braced and angry. "Who put you up to this? Do you think this is a *joke*?"

Mama tried to calm the nurse as the woman began to screech. I stared at the dead man and the dead man stared back. He smiled a crooked grin over crooked teeth. The dead man was gone with my next blink, as if he'd never been there at all.

Lesson 4: When the local hospital can't do anything for you and you've already got one incompetent triage nurse mightily pissed at you for speaking the truth, they'll ship you upstate. Every state has a hospital for non-Normies. Maybe it's tucked away among oaks or pine trees or not far from the beach, but every state except Delaware has a place for people like me. They have a spot reserved for you, too, if you aren't careful.

I'm not saying every person in charge of the mentally ill really knows the secret. Denial is a powerful thing. Denial can assure parents their son isn't gay so they won't have to disavow him. Denial lets us sleep at night when we could be acknowledging that the hey day for the human race is over and things are getting worse. However, some people know the truth and if you ever want to get out of those godforsaken green-tiled hospitals, you'll pretend to deny the truth, too. Don't be a whistleblower. You won't like it and I'll tell you why. The Powers That Be also fill those hospitals with genuinely crazy people. Before there were tinfoil hats, what *did* crazy people do to stop the command signals from the government, sentient reptiles and aliens from Alpha Centauri? Medicament's doctors diagnosed me as so crazy I'd need a tinfoil sombrero.

Then the well-meaning doctors of Medicament, Iowa sent me to Shibboleth Mental Hospital in Mason City. The admitting nurse was a nice woman named Sherry. Sherry's advantage, in my eyes, was that no dead people stood behind her, blaming her for their death.

My first roommate chewed her slippers to make them soft. She had bony tumors in the soles of her feet — yes, that's a thing — and she was convinced she'd be cured if she could just chew her shoes soft enough.

That was pretty benign compared to my other roommate. She had wild, tangled hair and wore no clothes and she stood against the wall, her arms up as if nailed in crucifixion. She never spoke. The dead are rarely overly chatty.

As soon as I walked into the room with its puke green, flaking paint, I knew this hospital was very old. I saw Petra and I froze. Just looking at her, I knew her name was Petra. She was Polish and no one on the staff had understood her. I don't understand how I knew, but she'd been placed in this hospital by mistake in 1972. Petra wanted to go home. She wanted her mama, too.

I also knew a secret was hidden beneath the drywall and buried behind the plaster. The old stone wall, back there in the dark, still bore the marks of where the chains were driven into the walls with huge flat spikes. This is where Petra was chained to a wall and raped by a young doctor named Moorely.

Lesson 5: when the man who raped a former patient turns out to be your doctor, you must escape that hospital. If flight isn't an option, that leaves fight.

# 3

The solution seemed simple. I told everyone my psychotic break from reality was over. *Ghosts? Zombies? Ghost zombies? What are you talking about? Who me?*

I thought I had a nurse on the hook, but Mama started crying and said, "Nobody's buying it, Tammy. You just don't want to be here. And I don't want to leave you here...but it's the right thing to do. I want you cured, okay? I want you *safe*. I love you so much, baby girl."

Mama's a strong woman. She left me in my room, despite me pleading to go back to Medicament and my dead armless boyfriend. When I called down the hall after her, Mama's last words to me were, "I'm from Amarillo."

Mama wouldn't have thought leaving me at Shibboleth Mental Hospital was such a good idea if she could see the naked girl reenacting the crucifixion.

The roommate who chewed her slippers told me everything would be okay and tried to stroke my hand. Her fingernails were dirty and bitten and chewed and wet. "I'm Rebecca Swift, but everybody calls me Becks," she said. "Everybody calls me Becks because they say I shoulda, woulda, coulda been a Spice Girl."

I soon found out no one called her Becks.

Then Rebecca lifted her bare feet to show me the bony tumors in the soles of her scarred feet again. "They cut 'em out and them little bones keep coming back."

You know your roommate is weird when you and the naked, dead, ghost girl give your roomie with foot tumors the same queasy look. I swear to God, when I caught Petra's eye, I almost laughed.

The next day I was ushered into a small office to meet my doctor. One side was lined with filing cabinets. The Venetian blinds were closed to sunshine and the man behind the battered metal desk sat in silhouette. A ring of smoke hung about his head. A small brass desk lamp cut through the smoke to make a small, nicotine-yellow circle of light on the papers that littered his desk.

"Miss...Smythe?"

"Tamara, yes."

"Did you sleep well?"

"Hardly at all."

"No one does. Not the first night. Tell me what brings you here."

I glanced at the open file spread before him. "I'm sure you've heard strange things. I thought I saw some things, but I was wrong. I had a rough time, but I'm better now."

"Well...you should pack your bags and go home, then, hm?"

"Really?"

"No."

Another silhouette appeared behind him. Her arms were at her side, but I couldn't miss that wild hair. Petra had been a pretty girl. Her head was cocked toward the man behind the desk. I knew who he must be.

The man leaned forward so the light from the desk lamp turned his eyeglasses into two yellow oval mirrors. "I am Dr. — "

"Moorely," I said.

"Yes. I am Dr. Jonathan Moorely. I'll be your psychiatrist during your stay with us. I only have two rules here. You're going to have to be honest with me and you must comply with my treatment plan, Tammy. I must insist. Do you understand?"

Past seventy now, with heavy bags under his red rimmed eyes, he sported a scraggly gray beard. He was the same man who raped Petra and he dared to demand honesty.

There were a lot of things I wanted to tell him, but none of it about me. I wanted to say, "I know what you did to Petra in 1972 in my room. It was before all the renovations were complete. The stone was cold on her back as you grabbed her hips. That was the last room untouched after they rebuilt, after the fire. That room should have been a museum piece, a tribute to psychiatry's dark history. Instead of disgusting you, those chains on the wall excited you. You wanted to use them before the reconstruction removed the old chains and covered up the sin."

"Miss Smythe? Cat got your tongue?"

"I'm fine, really."

"You seem distracted. Do you see your dead boyfriend in this room?"

"No. That would be crazy." I wanted to say, "You used those chains eighteen times, Dr. Moorely. You kept abusing her until that night, as you unchained her, after you were done, she smashed your glasses. There was a storm that night." I saw the lightning flashes strobe them as his fist rose and fell on her head, again and again.

"You beat her and she scratched you. As you stumbled away, she ate the broken glass. It took Petra three days to die."

"Miss Smythe? Do you hear voices? Do you have a plan to do harm to yourself or others?"

"No. Of course not."

*You,* I thought. *I will harm you.*

"Very well. I'm going to give you some more time to settle in. I'll also prescribe an anxiolytic." He wrote a note in my file.

"An anxio — "

"It will help calm you."

"I'm calm."

"You're sweating profusely although the room is cool. Your respirations are far too fast and the pulse in your lovely neck is racing. When you speak, you are almost breathless. Clearly, you are lying. I require honesty from my patients. We have to establish a therapeutic relationship and that is based on trust and open communication. Do you understand?"

"I guess."

"Guessing is not good enough."

"I do," I said.

I was supposed to say, "I do," to Brad. And now I was saying it to a rapist. My eyes were wet when an orderly came to lead me away to the common room.

I wondered how many helpless women he had abused over the years. Petra's eyes told me I wasn't the only one. Worse, her eyes told me I was next.

Dr. Moorely didn't come for me the first night. He managed to resist his impulses for three nights, as long as it took Petra to die. He came for me on my fourth night at Shibboleth Mental Hospital.

Which brings us to my only private black belt lesson with Mr. Stephen Chang. In case you forgot, we're up to Lesson Six. This might be the most important lesson and it's probably not what you're expecting.

# 4

**I** met Mr. Chang when I was eleven years old. I liked
Jackie Chan movies and I begged Mama to let me go to
his school in the middle of town. Medicament only has
one elementary school and one high school. Mr. Chang's
dojang was only a short walk down the street from the
schools.

"I need you around the pharmacy, girl," Mama said.
"Besides, what do you want to do? Hurt people?"

"No. I want to avoid getting hurt." That's what
changed her mind about letting me learn Hapkido.

Mr. Chang was an accountant when he wasn't teaching
martial arts. His mother was Korean and his father was
Chinese. "Some Chinese people and Koreans, historically,
hate each other," he said. "But any conflict can be
resolved when people are willing to listen to and respect
each other. However, when someone is unwilling to
respect you, that's why we learn Hapkido."

"To kick their ass?" a boy asked on the first day of class.

Mr. Chang laughed. "No. To blow off steam through
useful physical activity so we won't feel we have to hurt

them. We focus a lot here on conditioning before all else."

He lost a few prospective students that day. Those kids went to the edge of town to a karate studio in an industrial park, the one with all the tall golden trophies in the front window. I think his peaceful approach was one way Mr. Chang screened his students. He wanted the smart kids who didn't plan on bullying anyone with what he could teach them. "You can hurt someone with a throw. You can control someone with a joint lock. You can discourage them with kicks and punches. But use soft words first."

Sounds pretty Mr. Miyagi *Karate Kid* vanilla, doesn't it?

That's why my private lesson with Mr. Chang surprised me. One week after I was awarded my black belt, Mr. Chang told me to meet him at the dojang early on a Sunday morning. Brad's horrific death was still a couple of months away and I was pouring over college brochures, waiting to hear about scholarships from the universities Mama couldn't afford to send me to. My safety schools had already accepted me, but I was hoping for Northwestern.

Brad said I shouldn't go so far that he couldn't visit. He applied to universities in the same cities I did. He was going to take business and agriculture. We didn't think anything could stop us then. We hadn't counted on the hay baler. Nobody counts on the hay baler.

Mr. Chang greeted me at the door to the dojang. "Good morning, Ms. Smythe. Did you bring your sneakers?"

When I said I did, he pointed to his feet. "Me, too! Ready for a run?"

Mr. Chang often ran with his students to warm up

when the weather was good. The weather that early spring day was a cold, hard rain. He caught my glance out of the school's front windows. "We won't melt," he said.

"I was thinking we would freeze," I said.

"Not for a while. Not if we run hard enough."

And so we ran, first through town and then to the edge of Medicament. We kept going, side by side. If he had a destination in mind, he didn't tell me. After an hour, we were both drenched in sweat though the rain had soaked through our clothes. My breath was coming shallow and hard. Mr. Chang did not speak and gave no hint that he planned to slow the pace. The rain began to pour harder, bouncing off the macadam.

After more than an hour of hard running with lightning flashes in the distance, I finally asked, "Shouldn't we head back, sir?"

He stopped and signaled for me to rest. "Keep moving though. Your muscles will lock up and get hypothermic if you stop altogether. We probably should have headed back forty minutes ago."

My laugh was ragged. "Then why didn't we?"

"I was waiting to see how long it would take you to say we should turn back. You're a stubborn one. Do you know when to give up?"

"Mama's from Amarillo. She doesn't approve of giving up." I panted and swallowed thick phlegm. "Is this another test?"

He shook his head. "You passed black belt and earned it. It was a fine achievement. You are a very good student, Ms. Smythe. You put your all into the training. I fear you don't know when to quit, but perhaps there is a lot of Amarillo in you, as well."

"Thanks, sir. I think."

"I have few female students. I always have one private lesson with my female students after they achieve black belt. We need to talk about your most important lesson."

I was wary. "Okay."

"Come. Let's walk a while before the sprint back to the dojang."

"Yes, sir."

"Your boyfriend seems nice."

Mr. Chang often speaks in non sequiturs so I wasn't thrown. "Brad *is* nice."

"Good. When my mother brought my father home to meet her parents for the first time, my grandmother asked her, 'He treat you nice?' It seems like it should be an outdated question, doesn't it? I think young women better understand their worth now compared to my parents' time."

"I hope so."

"I've taught you a lot about defending yourself and you have learned very well. Did I ever tell you why I began teaching Hapkido?"

"You started by teaching your daughter, right?"

"Yes. Sasha. She's off at college now, not much older than you. Do you know why I started teaching her?"

"Was someone bothering her at school or something? Nothing too bad, I hope." My mind went to worst case scenaria, of course, and I worried that he was about to tell me some horrible story about an assault on his child.

"She is pre-diabetic," he said. "Are you familiar with the term?"

"Before diabetic, I guess."

"She's not full blown diabetic. Borderline. Many people

say that once one becomes pre-diabetic, diabetes is inevitable eventually. I set out to prove that wrong. I didn't want her to suffer the worry, health issues and expenses diabetes carries for life."

"So you got her doing Hapkido like your mother taught you?"

"No. I'm an accountant, too. I did research and came up with values for foods and put all the information into a spreadsheet, color coded."

"Did that help?"

"Some. Not enough. The doctor said that if she was to change her metabolism and get more sensitive to insulin, she must exercise and make sure she sweats when she works out at least 30 minutes each day. I was very concerned for her, so I made her work out two hours a day."

"How'd that go?"

"She is healthy and is no longer considered pre-diabetic. She has a second-degree black belt now."

"That's wonderful."

He smiled. "My daughter does not speak to me."

"I don't understand."

"She did not want to exercise. She did not want to be my first student. I started the dojang purely for her benefit. When I learned Hapkido, I was only interested in learning for my benefit, to protect myself from all the evils of the world. I had no interest in teaching. Then I thought if Sasha had other students with whom to compete and endure the training with, she would embrace the spirit of the trial. It was hard for her. She thinks I am too hard on her."

"Even now?"

"Over time, the lessons about food and regular exercise became normal for her, but she resented me for being such a taskmaster. She is studying engineering in California now. We talk on her birthday and Christmas. It is…awkward."

"I'm sorry. It's not fair to you."

"I *was* very hard on her, much as I am demanding of you," he admitted. "People talk a lot about what's fair, Ms. Smythe. They confuse the way they want things to be with the way they are. We must make the world we want. I am not sorry about training Sasha for a better life. I did the right thing. My daughter will live a longer and, ultimately, a happier life because I was willing to do what was necessary."

"Happier without you?"

"People say that, after a time, we do not miss what is not there. I'm hoping that's true. I still miss my daughter. Perhaps not enough time has gone by yet. Maybe she will realize she misses me before much longer." He shrugged. "I do not worry about the things I cannot control and those things that are under my control require no worry."

A moment of silence passed and I thought he was going to say I was like a daughter to him, or something sappy like that. Again, he surprised me. "You have to be willing to do what others will not do. To make more money, you must be willing to do things others will not. My brother owns a waste disposal business in Austin. His trucks haul away medical waste. No one wants to do that. That's why my brother owns two houses and a boat. And take me. So many of my clients hate doing taxes. They look at a column of numbers and a pile of receipts and they panic every April. I get the most money out of those who panic.

They come in with bags of receipts and I have to figure out what they did all year. Those who lack discipline think they are taking the easy way out, but they always end up paying more one way or another."

"So, is that the lesson, sir? You want me to keep track of my receipts?"

He laughed and motioned for me to run with him again. A car drove around us and a wide puddle. The driver avoided the opportunity to splash us at high speed and we both waved our thanks to the driver.

"I'm telling you this, Ms. Smythe, because life is hard and you're young enough to think it isn't all that bad. To survive, sometimes you must do what others will not. For instance, your kata is excellent. You do the drills, all with precision and power. But you need to know, if you are attacked by a larger person who knows good fighting technique, you are at a distinct disadvantage."

"That's why we do Hapkido. To even the odds."

"If you are fighting to survive, even odds are not enough. If you are in a fair fight, you have not planned correctly. You must be willing to do what others won't. When two men of similar weight fight, who is more likely to win, Ms. Smythe?"

This was a question from one of my first lessons. I answered without thinking, "The one most likely to win is the one who strikes first. Aggression often works."

"Yes. And when a man fights a woman, his goal is usually to control her. That is your advantage. If a man tries to hit you, what is your goal?"

"Stop him. Create distance. Get away. Get help."

"And if you can't do those things?"

"Why wouldn't I? I've got skills — "

"Dangerous thinking, Ms. Smythe. I'm not talking about a tournament or a friendly sparring match. You will soon go out into the world. Leave behind childish ideas about working out on the mat in the dojang with your friends. Your opponent is willing to beat you until you are unconscious. He'll try to strangle you. He doesn't just think he's tough. He *is* tough. What must you do?"

"I must...do what he is unwilling to do?"

"Are you asking me or are you telling me?"

"I must do what he is unwilling to do, sir."

"And what is that?"

He was the accountant, but I did the math. I knew the answer he was looking for, even though I didn't really believe him then. Not yet. "Kill him," I answered.

"That is your advantage. No self-defense training is complete without acknowledging this. I've taught you kicks and punches and locks and throws. More powerful than all of these are the simple things we do instinctively when our lives are threatened. As Bruce Lee said, 'Poke out their eyes, punch 'em in the balls, take out their knees.' Simple and direct. If you are prepared to be brutal, you will survive. The words to remember belong to Malcolm X. 'By any means necessary.'"

We ran a long time before we spoke again. The rain had eased but my legs were tired and beginning to cramp. I had trained for short bursts of speed and strength in Hapkido practice, not long distance running. The cold ached down to my bones and my breath came short through clenched teeth.

"Are you telling me I've been wasting my time with you since I was eleven years old?" I asked.

He laughed. "No, Ms. Smythe. Now you know

27

everything you need to know in order to defend yourself well. Everything else was preparation. To defend ourselves, we must be in good physical condition. We must be willing to do terrible things. Finally, we must be relatively calm in order to do those terrible things to defend ourselves…and others."

"Can we rest a while?" I asked.

"No."

"I'm thirsty."

"Of course. It's raining. Tip your head back, open your mouth and drink."

We ran on. He was used to running and I wasn't and it showed. Despite being twenty years younger, it was all I could do to stay at his heels. I fell twice before we got back to the dojang and he did not slow. He expected me to catch up. When I did so without complaining, my reward at the door to the school was a smile and a bow.

"That concludes our private lesson, Ms. Smythe. Please remind your mother that your dues are required at the first of the month. Do you need a ride home?"

I desperately wanted a ride home in a warm car. "No, thank you, sir."

"Good run, Ms. Smythe."

"Good run, sir."

"Oh, and Ms. Smythe? One more thing. If you do find it necessary to kill anyone, I will be your character witness at the trial."

"Great."

"Just be sure you win."

The truth is, I didn't really pay Mr. Chang that much attention at the time. I took him seriously, but I chalked up his stern pronouncements to OCD and maybe watching too many old Jackie Chan movies where the master is avenged by his student prodigy.

I didn't really believe that life was that hard. At least, not until Life ended and Death took Brad away from me.

Mr. Chang's edict was much on my mind as I left Dr. Moorely's office. The way he looked at me and the words, "your lovely neck," haunted me more than Petra's wild hair, gray naked body and scarred wrists.

# 5

Lesson 7: when trapped in a mental hospital designed to make you conform to expected societal norms, do the expected.

When you suspect the old serial rapist doctor may prescribe you a heavy sedative to make you compliant, don't put up a fuss. When the Powers That Be underestimate you, that's one of your few advantages.

When the nurse gives you the medication, don't try what actors do in movies. Unless it's the floor nurse's first day on the job and she has terrible training, she will ask you to swallow the prescribed pill. Then she'll ask you to stick out and lift your tongue. Hiding the big white capsule under your tongue is something that would only work in a movie.

The best way to appear to take the roofie (the deep sedative known as Rohypnol) is to palm it when the nurse hands it to you. Pantomime swallowing the pill and wince a little to sell the idea that you're a good little patient. However, this is dangerous and an old, savvy nurse will watch your hands, too. I wouldn't try this strategy unless your last name is Penn, Teller or Copperfield.

The easiest way to defeat Dr. Pervert's prescription is to actually take it. Show them you're not going to be any trouble. As soon as you can, without being obtrusive, slip into the bathroom and stick your fingers down your throat. Puke that puppy up and down into the toilet. Better fingers down your throat than something else.

Lesson 8: when the bedtime routine begins, watch your roomie (not the dead one.) Rebecca Call-Me-Becks will be out like a light because Dr. Moorely will want her passed out and snoring early, too.

When the lights go out, listen to the movement around the floor. Hospitals are like every other building. After the day's routines are done, they settle into a quieter pattern. Shifts change. The skeleton staff spreads thin, gets sleepy and moves less.

Patients who wander in the night pad the hallways in their bare feet and must be led back to bed. Nurses walk miles so they wear sneakers and squeak down the hall. The doctors' smooth dress shoes click a little on the tile in the corridor as they approach.

Do you hear those shoes clicking up and down the hall slowly, pacing? That's Dr. Moorely, building up his nerve. How many times he took advantage of his position in this hospital is impossible to know. You can be sure he has committed this atrocity many times. Every sex offender claims the time they were caught is the first time. We all know it's merely the last time — at least we hope it's the last time. Sex offenders typically keep at their sick obsessions for a long time until they are captured or killed.

As the steps outside my door became slower and more deliberate, Dr. Moorely gathered his courage (or succumbed to his impulses.) When he was certain it was safe and the snoring emanating from Call-Me-Becks' thin nose and thick, phlegmy throat was sure and even, he opened the door to the room.

Before he did that, I watched my roomie (the dead one). As I knew she would, Petra appeared, a pale crucifix against the wall that hid the marks of chains. Her eyes were deep black shadows, but a slant of weak light from the door caught glistening tears on her marble white cheeks. Blood dripped from her open mouth but no liquid hit the floor. She was terrified and, for some reason I can't understand, condemned to repeat this ritual until Dr. Moorely was stopped.

That's where I came in.

Lesson 9: This is a tough one. Pretend to sleep. I did. The toughest part was feeling his icy gaze on me. He slowly pulled back the sheet, on guard for me to stir, trying to gauge the depth of my Rohypnol sleep.

I waited for his pants to fall to his ankles so he'd be off balance when I shoved him down. When he crashed to the floor, I rolled up quick and leapt high in the air to land on the old man's stomach with both knees as hard as I could.

Moorely wheezed and could not get his breath. A rib cracked. With my pillow over his face, no air in his lungs and my weight on his ribs, he could not scream for help. If I kept the pillow pressed tight, he'd eventually stop struggling and would die of asphyxiation.

My plan was not to murder Dr. Moorely, though if he'd had a heart attack just then, I would not have objected. My plan was to take his eyes if need be. Mr. Chang and Petra would approve and, given the way Petra died, there was some poetic justice in maiming him that way.

Killing made it sound like I was doing something wrong. From Petra's experience, I was certain I was in the right. Still, I'd never killed anyone. Not yet. And I decided I preferred the term *dispatch*. The word suggested I was about to send the doctor somewhere. Perhaps he could roam these halls for decades on end, trapped in his own hell as Petra had been.

Lesson 10: I realized that, despite Mr. Chang's private lesson, I wasn't ready to dispatch anyone, not even this sick bastard. The first kill is the hardest and I wasn't ready to be an executioner.

What to do? *What to do?*

Then I saw my way out. I spotted the rectangular square of foil wrapper by his outstretched hand. In the dim light, the pills looked black, but by their shape and, guessing at his age, I knew what pills the doctor had readied for himself.

I leaned down and bit his ear hard to get his attention and he startled, letting out the barest of moans. I was sweating and my heart pounded, but Chang was right. All that training under stress worked. All things considered, I was relatively calm and prepared for battle.

"I only have two rules, Doctor. You must be honest with me and you must comply with my treatment plan. For every pill you swallow," I said, "I'll allow you to take two deep breaths, one before and one after. I must insist. Do you understand?"

He struggled under me, so I drew back one knee and drove my bony kneecap into his balls hard. I felt the squish and my stomach turned over. His eyes widened so much I could see the whites all the way around his pupils. The old man *squeaked*.

While he was still thinking about his ruined testicles, I lifted the other knee and brought all my weight down into his diaphragm.

Chang was right: to defend ourselves, we must be in good physical condition. I had little to fear from a seventy-year-old predator who used drugs to subdue his victims.

I explained what he was going to do and, of course, he wanted to protest. But he needed air for that. He nodded weakly and we began. He ate one blue pill. I guessed he'd already taken one or two. The box in his breast pocket contained two foil packages. I took the pen from that same pocket and shoved the point up against his carotid artery. He swallowed every pill dry. That took a while, but Call-me-Becks was in a deep snore so there was no rush.

Petra put her arms down and stepped closer. The ghost girl's feet were coated in filth and trails of dried blood ran black as they wound down her legs in the moonlight. Her proximity freaked me out but, when I glanced up, the ghost's head was cocked to one side. Her look communicated all the uncomprehending curiosity of a dog staring at a ceiling fan.

I focused on the doctor. When he was done taking his medicine, I could tell the pills had their intended effect. I wanted to throw up in his face, but I'd watched a lot of CSI with Brad. It's a mistake to vomit at a crime scene and I still didn't know how this was going to work out.

"Two packets. That's ten pills, Dr. Moorely. Do you know what happens next?"

He shook his head weakly.

"Oh, I think you do." I knew what was coming down the train track with Moorely tied to the rails. Mama owned Medicament's only pharmacy and I helped out on weekends for years. I'd read the labels and giggled over the potential side effects of drugs since I was thirteen years old.

I gave Dr. Moorely a fierce sneer. "First, there's an excellent chance your heart will give out as you limp out into the hallway. I can feel your pulse in your lovely neck, Doctor, pounding away. It feels like your heart is about to explode. You shouldn't smoke. It's bad for you."

His eyes were wet. I looked around for some pity but couldn't find any. Not with Petra standing over us, watching justice get served.

"If you make it to the nurses' station, there's a good chance you'll die of embarrassment."

He struggled for breath. "Listen to m— "

"*Sh!* You'll wake the baby." I pressed his pen harder into his throat and he shut up. I wondered what Brad would say. He was always pithy and funny in a crisis. My zombie boyfriend was a sharp guy. For instance, though he suddenly found himself disarmed, Brad had thought to use a pencil to dial the phone before he died. He'd thought to call me one last time, with a special message that might be true love's last sad gift. Or it might be a curse.

"We're going to wait until dawn, Doctor. We'll make sure all those little pills take full effect. We won't be using them. We're just going to have to wait. You've seen the commercials. If you have an erection lasting longer than four hours, consult a doctor immediately. It's six, maybe seven hours to morning. They'll have to operate, I think. It'll be fractured and broken because, a little later, after you pass out, I'm going to wake you up by driving my knees into your penis. I don't care how long it takes. Petra's been waiting a long time for justice. We can give her one night of our lives."

At the mention of her name, Dr. Moorely's eyes narrowed. He managed to whisper, "How do you know that name?"

"If I told you, you'd lock me up in an insane asylum, Doctor."

# 6

It was a long night and, if I had to do it again, I would have drunk more coffee. On the other hand, I'd already peed on him plenty. It's hard to hold someone down that long, harder than a hard run in a cold rain.

When the wait for the sun's return got boring, I reminded myself that Petra had been trapped here since 1972.

Lesson 11: when you're holding an old man down with all your weight and strength, definitely make full use of the threat of the pen tip at his throat. Otherwise, when he surrenders, he's actually resting, waiting for his chance at escape.

I spent the night feeling for his muscles to tense against mine. I spent the night threatening him. My knees ached. My back hurt. The muscles in my jaw went into spasms before it was over. The ghost of Petra stood watch over me through the night, mute but, I felt, encouraging.

The memory of Mr. Chang kept me going, too. I could hear him saying, "If you give this man a chance, he will kill you."

That was true. Pain gave Moorely fear. However, as the dawn spread light into the room slowly, I saw the hatred boiling behind his eyes ever more clearly.

I got so tired toward the end, he almost pushed me off and circled his hands around my throat. That's very dangerous. Blood vessels burst in your eyes. If you strangle someone the right way, focusing on the blood vessels to the victim's brain instead of trying to close their airway, it doesn't take long to choke someone unconscious.

About the time he slipped one hand around my neck I realized I'd done this all wrong. I should have piled my sheets and pillows in the bed as a decoy. I should have slipped behind the door and waited. Then I could have jumped on his back and choked him out and tied him up instead of spending the whole night holding him down and counting my muscle spasms to pass the time.

What can I say? I was new at this sort of thing.

The room that had been painted yellow with sunlight a moment before he began to choke me. Then the room began to darken. I dropped the pen from his throat and he had me, squeezing with both hands. I tried to pull my head back and, for a moment, I saw Petra's wild, pleading eyes. She shook her head.

I threw my head forward but he stopped me from headbutting him. The old man had been resting a while and saw his last chance.

Then I saw my last chance. With the last of my strength, I clapped my hands over his ears and burst his ear drums. His eyes rolled up and his mouth popped open.

"Enough," he wheezed. "Enough!"

Call-Me-Becks snorted awake in time to see me put both hands on the floor on either side of Moorely's head, rock forward and kick my cramped legs straight in the air into a handstand. When my knees came down, I fulfilled my promise, fracturing what would never again point straight. I rolled off Moorely and rolled toward the wall. Petra's wall. I cried and wailed and screamed for help and squeaky nurses' shoes pounded the green linoleum.

I was almost unconscious from exhaustion, but I saw Petra looking down at me. She had a nice smile. She lifted a hand (to wave goodbye, I think.) I noticed it was clean. She had not a spot of dirt or a dribble of blood on her body.

I blinked and she wasn't there anymore. Makes you wonder what's happening while you're doing all that blinking every day, doesn't it?

Dr. Moorely missed his window of opportunity for an easy fix for his little problem. A simple needle in his needle dick would have drained that painful, broken erection. They tried to save his weapon of choice. However, two days later, gangrene set in. A surgeon in another hospital down the road detached the diseased organ from the control of Moorely's diseased mind.

The old man retired amid many questions. The hospital administrator wanted to know what he was doing in the women's wing of the hospital, alone after midnight. The DA wanted to know what he was doing with all that Viagra in his pocket. The police wanted to know why he'd prescribed unusually heavy doses of sleeping pills for me and my (live) roommate that night.

I thought the case would go to trial, but three weeks later, disgraced and dickless, Dr. Moorely took his life. He did it at home with a pistol to the forehead.

A very nice detective came to see me after Moorely

killed himself. Owens was his name. Detective Owens told me he had a daughter about my age so, as far as he was concerned, my actions were self-defense.

"I could have called for the nurses," I said.

"No, you couldn't," Detective Owens said. "He was crazy, overdosed on Viagra and he threatened to kill you if you called for help."

I watched his eyes as I nodded. "Yeah," I said. "That's about right."

"What's not right about it?" Owens asked.

Then I told him everything. He took no notes. He didn't believe my story, of course. He should have. He was the only one to whom I told the entire truth, including everything I knew about Petra. I was already in a mental hospital. My defense was insanity. Given where I was, that seemed airtight.

Owens watched me for a long time after I finished. "Tamara, do you plan to hurt anyone else?"

"Not unless they come at me with a loaded weapon like Dr. Moorely did."

He nodded.

"It was self-defense," Owens said. "He overdosed on the pills himself. You didn't scream because you were afraid for your life and your roommate's life. The bruises on your neck tell the only story I need to know. Do you understand?"

"Yes."

"That's how my report will read."

"Okay."

"And you will never tell anyone everything you just told me. Dr. Moorely told you about Petra. He taunted you with her memory. You did not see her that night.

Understand?"

"Thank you, Detective Owens."

The hospital administrators didn't want the truth getting out, either. Depositions dragged out in court and before the media would be too embarrassing. They wanted the scandal over and done with quickly. I received a decent settlement. Hush money, Mama called it. The lawyers for the hospital said that if I exposed the fact that one of their doctors had abused patients for decades it would besmirch the institution. People who needed help wouldn't feel safe coming there anymore.

"Well, *boo-hoo*. We *weren't* safe, were we?" I said.

I signed the agreement on condition they would discharge me immediately to Mama's custody. The hospital promised to investigate to try to find more victims. Given the vulnerable population they served at Shibboleth, I doubt they ever turned up another of Moorely's prey.

Petra and I certainly weren't the only victims. I know that (and it's logical given the patterns of sexual predators as taught to me by *CSI Miami*.) But for some reason, Petra was the only one who showed up on my ghost radar. Was it because she was his first victim, because she died there or because, like me, she was sane in an insane situation?

The details of Dr. Moorely's suicide were not made public. Unless it's a celebrity who kills themselves, the media's rule is to avoid inspiring copycats. Why it's okay to inspire people to kill themselves after a celeb takes his own life is one of those unanswerable mysteries. It's the gap between what's smart and what's done. That gap is everywhere if you start to look around.

Anyway, I saw Dr. Moorely again. On the day I left the

hospital I looked up from my bed and jumped and shrieked. The old man stood before me in an open, bloody robe wearing nothing underneath it. You can use your imagination about what was left between his legs. You won't need much imagination.

Moorely stared at me. I saw his fury again. He walked into the room and lay on the floor. A small, red hole gaped in the middle of his forehead. The back of his head was an empty mess of red, white and gray mash. Dr. Moorely stared at the ceiling and wept silently, tears streaming down his face, his arms outstretched as if on a cross.

My bags were already packed. When I left that room for the last time, I stepped over him as if he wasn't there. Call-Me-Becks stayed on her bed, rubbing the bony tumors in her feet and chewing the soles of her slippers.

It was brutal therapy, but I have to confess, I wasn't quite as scared of ghosts anymore.

Lesson 12: Psychiatry works!

# 7

Lesson 13: no matter how straightforward the easy answer is, there will always be a skeptic trying to tell you that your life transforming experience didn't really happen.

For instance, as soon as I got out of the hospital, I got Mama to drive us to Piggly Wiggly's. Ten minutes later, we sat at a rest stop off Highway 65, hashing it out over ham sandwiches and Cokes. Mama had a lot of questions, but I didn't have many answers that satisfied her.

After about the fifth time of her asking if I was okay, I started to cry. "How can I be okay? What does all this mean?"

Her troubled look told me she didn't have a lot of answers that would satisfy me, either. When I asked Mama if she believed my story, she said she believed that I believed my story. That was *very* unsatisfying.

"With Brad's death, you've been through a lot, Tammy. What if you've got...I mean, what if this is PTSD?"

"Like what soldiers get?"

"Sure."

"Mama, I loved Brad with all my heart, but are you

honestly going to sit there and tell me I got Post-traumatic Stress Disorder from my boyfriend's death? I mean, if that's true, wouldn't everybody get it?"

"Well…maybe you got it from your fight with the doctor."

It was my turn to play skeptic. "If fights and funerals made it that easy to get PTSD, who *wouldn't* have it?"

"I'm sorry, baby. I just…think PTSD sounds more logical and maybe preferable to the other possibilities."

"Like what possibilities? I saw Ghost Zombie Brad before I saw Naked Petra, and before Dr. McPervy Bad Touch came into my hospital room."

"Maybe we should see another doctor. Get some more opinions. Y'know, just to rule things out."

"You think I have a brain tumor or something?"

"No, Tammy! No! But…."

"What?"

"Schizophrenia might be something we should rule out."

I lost my appetite for ham sandwiches and took three long swallows of my Coke. I wished it was on ice. I wished I had loaded up on sugar. Girls joke about dealing with a bad breakup by chowing down on Haagen Dazs butter pecan ice cream in a bathtub. Double Stuf Fudgee-os are my drug of choice and, boy, did I crave my medicine. (The *Stuf* part really is spelled with one *f*, which gives you something else to ponder when the box is empty too soon, the sugar crash comes and you hate yourself.)

"Do you think I have what Daddy had?" I asked.

Mama looked terrified. "We don't really know what your father had, Tammy. He didn't stick around long enough for us to find out. But no. Definitely not!"

"You always called him crazy. You think I've got the crazy gene, too, don't you?"

"Why do you say these things?"

"Because if you didn't think I was crazy, I think you'd look less scared."

"He wasn't crazy, exactly, Tammy. He withdrew. And… yes…he had visions. He said he wasn't meant for this world."

Mama had told me the story many times. She told it the long way. I'll give you the short version: When Daddy said he wasn't meant for this world, Mama thought he meant to kill himself. Maybe he just meant he wasn't meant for our little part of the world. He left Iowa. He disappeared one day and left the divorce papers, already drawn up, in the mailbox. The forwarding address was in Brooklyn.

"You are not your father. Can't be. That would be too...*too*."

"Too *what?*"

"Just too."

"Just, too, too *what*, Mama?"

"Unfair. Too much and too unfair."

She looked at the sky as if the clouds would form letters to spell out some reassuring answers to her questions. Her hope for a world where bad things only happened to bad people was the chasm between us. I was jealous of Mama in that moment. She'd somehow held on to that belief even as Brad's death ripped my hope away.

*Unfairness.* Mr. Chang had warned me about thinking too much about what's fair.

"Fair in a fight or fair in life?" I'd asked Mr. Chang.

"Same, same," Mr. Chang had replied.

Petra sure didn't get much of a taste of what's fair. Mr.

Chang was right. Life is hard. Death is even harder.

Mama shook her head and wiped away a tear but I barreled on. "If you could have been there and seen the girl, you'd know I'm not making this up or anything. And what about the triage nurse back in Medicament? She didn't know that poor man was having a heart attack until it was too late. I hit a nerve with her, bang on, didn't I?"

"We don't know what happened there, Tammy."

"We don't, but I do."

"Okay."

"Okay, what?"

"Okay," she said. "I believe you."

"Why? Because you don't want to believe I take after my father?"

"I believe you because you're *my* daughter. Whatever was in him that you might have inherited, half of you still comes from me."

She hugged me but I wasn't done being mad at her so I didn't hug her back.

"Tammy? Besides coming from Amarillo, I was brought up Presbyterian. What do ghosts mean for the big picture?"

"What big picture?"

"Heaven. Hell. Death. Life, the universe and everything. I haven't been a good Presbyterian," Mama said. "I mean, I always wanted to believe in heaven, but as a pharmacist, I have questions about how the real world works and it butts up against my Bible. And now? I don't know what to think. If Death isn't necessarily the end… well, that's what we're all hoping for, isn't it? Salvation. But, with ghosts, if it isn't a real new beginning, either…. I just don't know what to think now. If there are ghosts wandering around just looking in on us all the time, I'm gonna have to start showering with my clothes on, at least until I lose a little weight."

I managed to laugh at that. "I don't have all the answers, Mama. I don't know about the big picture. I'm just trying to get through the day."

"You've been a very strong girl and you know I'm proud of you. Even so, Dr. Moorely's death must have been a shock, even for a strong girl."

That's when I understood that Mama didn't understand me. Her genteel rules said I was somehow supposed to feel at least a little bad for Moorely. We were supposed to think he was sick. Mama thought I should feel guilt for the wounds I inflicted, especially if they led to the old pervert killing himself. The truth was, I felt nothing but hate for him. *Glad* he was dead? No. *Ecstatic* is the right word.

People who don't feel sympathy for others are monsters. Mama worried that I didn't abide by her expectations to express some kind of regret. I never said I was sorry. It was necessary to hurt the doctor badly, so I did. If I'd called the nurses, the situation might have devolved into a he said, she said sort of thing. When I looked in Petra's eyes, I knew I couldn't let that happen. I didn't share Mama's worries that I'd become a monster. In fact, I did feel plenty of compassion for others. I felt deep empathy for Petra. All my sympathy went out to her so I had nothing left for Moorely.

I didn't blame Mama for her worries. She was brought up a sweet Southern gal. Mama had not seen the look of fear and pain in Petra's eyes. When my dead roommate stood naked against the wall with half circles of bite marks across her breasts and trailing down her belly, I felt her horror. When she escaped the trap of that room, I felt her elation.

I thought of Brad then. How could I release him? Was it really me who was keeping him from going... somewhere?

That's Lesson 14, I guess. We don't know what happens after death, but the dead don't know any better, either. They're still stuck, half in and half out of this plane of existence. Most, not all, are like Petra, hoping for a connecting flight to what Mama calls the Happy Hunting Grounds.

Brad was a good young man. The only sin I ever knew he committed was lust. He committed that sin with me and when it's that good it can't be bad. Why he was condemned to stay, I did not know. I only saw him in two places: in the backyard outside my window and in the field, standing amid the tall grasses. I felt he was waiting for something that he could only get from me, but he either didn't or couldn't say what that special ticket to ride might be.

When Mama and I finished our sandwiches from Piggly Wiggly's and drained our Cokes, she asked me what I wanted to do next. Given my farm boy boyfriend's trap, I knew I would not return to Medicament. I had some money now. Mama assumed I would go to university and restart my life, fresh and Bradless. That wouldn't have been fresh enough for me. I wasn't about to go quiz the clergy or run away to hide at a retreat at a yoga ashram and live off brown rice and tofu, either. Nothing against yoga. I like how my bum looks in yoga pants. As for the clergy, I figured that I already knew more about life after death than most.

What I chose next might seem a little weird. Until recently, I'd thought I possessed a scientific mind. Maybe I still did because I told Mama, "It's time to experiment."

It was also time to run far away. What's a girl with money do instead of getting drunk in a dorm for Frosh week? A normal girl might go to Hawaii or Miami or Aspen. I decided to move to New York City.

Mama looked distraught and a little angry at the same time. "No, not there, Tammy. Please."

I told Mama I had two simple reasons: A. It was far from my loitering farm boy boyfriend. B. I'd never been to New York City and it sounded exciting.

I had an ulterior motive, also. C. That's where my father ran off to. I told Mama I wouldn't go near Brooklyn and that I had no interest in tracking him down. I'm sure she knew I was lying but I think she appreciated the effort.

Lesson 15: When you tell your Mama you're leaving for a long trip and you don't know when or maybe even if you'll come back, hug her. Squeeze her extra tight when she cries.

"I don't think New York is the place to put all this ugliness behind you," Mama said. "Promise me that if you see something, just let it be. Don't get dragged into anything. No more Dr. Moorelys. Just pretend you don't see it and move on. You can pretend."

She didn't say, "Pretend to be a Normie," but it seemed like a perfectly reasonable strategy at the time. Of course, I tried. Good thing I failed. If I'd succeeded, you wouldn't be reading this guide to surviving Armageddon.

# 8

Lesson 16: Most of the dead move on to wherever they're going. Heaven? Hell? Maybe they go no more than six feet down. I don't know, but most of the dead have an address elsewhere. If the stiffs all stayed, the streets and sidewalks of New York would be much more crowded than they already are. The dead would be everywhere in various states of dress and undress, creeping me out at every turn. There are plenty of ghosts around, but the math suggests the ones who remain among us are outliers.

Lesson 17: ghosts seem to stay for lots of reasons. Not all of them are gritting their teeth about their grizzly murders, lost loves or unsolved mysteries. Not all ghosts are trapped. Some, I think, are lazy. Others seem to hang on and hang out for nostalgic reasons. Maybe the rest are just curious about what happens next in a world that's moving on without them. We're all curious about what the future holds. I think that's true even for those who don't have a future here anymore. Maybe some are scared to leave.

I was scared to stay in Iowa, so I took the train to New

York. After being locked up at Shibboleth, it was a relief to sit by myself by the window and watch the world go by. Mama wanted to come with me. I told her she had already missed too much time away from the pharmacy. She had to get back to Medicament and back to work.

Mama argued, of course. Then I told her she couldn't come to New York. "You weren't going to come babysit me when I went off to university, so there's no reason to come now."

"But it's New York City," she said.

"And I'm me. I'll be fine. Besides, you have to go make sure Kelly isn't drunk with power and annoying the cashiers so much they quit. It's a small town. We don't have a big pool of cashiers to draw from."

That was true, and just the right button to push with my mother. Kelly Keegan, Mama's store manager, managed the paperwork, taxes and payroll well, but wasn't meant to be in charge of human beings. She was meant to be hidden away in a back office, far from the customers (whom Kelly despised) and away from the staff (at whom she routinely sniffed, reminding them that, if they wanted a raise or time off, they were replaceable.)

Mama gave a resigned nod. "You're right. Kelly will have them all in knots and doing deep knee bends just to mess with them."

"Go, Mama. The cashiers need you. That woman is a tyrant if you aren't around. But Kelly Keegan doesn't mess with Texas."

"You're goddamn right," Mama said. "Excuse my French."

Before I went out on the train platform to leave Iowa and seek my fortune in the big city, Mama and I made small talk about the drugstore. It was a relief to talk about normal things. All the while, I pretended I didn't see the man in the vintage train conductor's uniform pacing the train station. The dead man looked far too pale and twice as fussy, comparing the time on his pocket watch to the station's big clock and staring down the tracks impatiently.

As passengers were called to board the train, I kissed Mama's cheeks and tasted the salt of her tears.

"Don't worry, Mama. I know what I'm doing."

You have to be really young and dumb to have that kind of confidence. Fortunately, when you're that young and naive, dumb protects you from the truth of your odds of winning. For a while.

Lesson 18: Mundane is good. If your life is boring, you aren't being tormented by bad people and dead people aren't vying for your attention. People say they want exciting lives, but most excitement comes from things going horribly wrong in new and surprising ways. By that measure, I lead an exciting life.

As my train slid out of the station and headed east, I watched the landscape. Flax seed, red clover, rye and wheat shimmered in sunlight. I saw no dead cows or dead boyfriends standing like daydreaming sentinels amid the hay.

Lesson 19: The movie title is true. All dogs go to heaven. Or at least they don't stay here. I've never seen a ghost who hadn't once walked the earth on two legs. Animals seem to die and that's it for them here. Cats don't stay to haunt the litterbox and prowl the backyard. Maybe, to be a ghost, you need a higher level of self-absorption (though it's hard to imagine creatures more self-absorbed than cats. I love them, but they know we're here to serve them.)

My guess is that ghosts require a higher level of sentience to stay among the living. Or maybe the ghost dead have a bit more narcissism than the rest of the departed dead. To die and to choose the half-existence between worlds is to fail to imagine an Earth that could go on successfully without you.

I transferred trains in Chicago — the Capitol Limited to the Northeast Regional. I had a new iPad in my backpack courtesy of the attempted sexual assault settlement. I had the latest iPhone in my pocket, courtesy of Mama. She told me to call her every night. I negotiated until I convinced her texting would make my money last longer. Mostly, I just stared out of my window and watched the country roll by.

Lesson 20: if you, like me, see the dead, you'll wonder why Fate chose you to see things you shouldn't. Did you fall out of bed one night and hit your head on the floor hard enough to flick a switch? Or maybe you picture something more Disney, like a curse by an evil witch.

My advice is to follow Mr. Chang's advice. Don't worry about what you can't control. At first, getting haunted always feels like a curse. How could it not? We're told how the world works and then one day we discover there's much more going on than we thought.

Worse? The dead are bothersome. They have no boundaries. They'll interrupt you at any time, day or night, to plague you with explicit visions and cryptic messages. Also, they stare a lot, which is both rude and off-putting.

For reasons unknown (perhaps most of them are damned) it's hard for many of them to communicate with us. They rarely seem to talk to each other much or maybe they aren't even aware of each other. Maybe that's more ghost narcissism.

Sometimes it seems to me it's as if they're shouting across too wide a chasm to reach us with desperate messages. Most of what I hear from the dead comes in short, emotion-laden bursts: word pictures, an ominous feeling, longing looks. Occasionally you will run into dead people who can speak plainly, which is always interesting…at first. Typically, they ruin it by not knowing when to shut up. Ghosts walk among us all day and night, after all. (The dead do not sleep and there's a good chance one of them is looking over your shoulder, reading these words right now.) After being ignored by the Normies for so long, it's natural, given the chance to gab, they tend to spew.

(If you are a ghost reading this, sorry, no offense meant. Don't play with the lights or mess with the reader after the lights go out, please. I'm just saying.)

My point is, the dead need therapy and if they sense you can hear them, they choose you without any care for your personal life. Sometimes my life feels like I'm trying to watch my favorite television show and ghosts are toddlers running in front of the screen, trying to get my attention.

Which brings us to Lesson 21. It's an important one. People who see the dead have all seen *The Sixth Sense*. If we had meetings and formed a union, our motto would be, "Yes, I see dead people. Now leave me alone!" What the kid in the movie didn't get is that you can't unsee dead people, but you *can* pretend they aren't there. I recommend you ignore them as much as possible.

When you think about it, our world is built on pretend and make believe. Human rights is something we made up. Human rights aren't real — life's not fair, remember — but we do try to live by those make believe rules. We pretend our votes count. We pretend the dead couldn't possibly be standing behind us, peering over our shoulders, reading along with you as you flip through this manual.

I didn't get this at first. Sometimes a ghostly presence is so close and strong, you can't help but react to them. That's when they know they have you. Acknowledging their existence seems to make most of them think you owe them something. Therefore, if you want to be left alone by the dead, do your best to go on doing what you did before you got the power. Look busy and focused as if the boss is breezing through the office.

Lesson 22: you won't *always* be able to pretend they aren't there. Everybody wants something and the dead are no exception. What do the dead want? They want what everyone wants. They want attention. The ones who manage to work themselves up so much that they can throw things around and rearrange the furniture? That's a temper tantrum from somebody who's tired of being ignored. If you even glance a ghost's way and they sense a glimmer of recognition, they can really be a pain in the ass.

Which brings up Lesson 23, I guess. We better delve deeper into how to avoid misty wistfuls. (That's what some of us non-Normies call ghosts: the Misty Wistfuls. Poetic, huh? I can play classical piano, but if I had a little indie coffeehouse band, I'd call it the Misty Wistfuls.)

You know all those stories of poltergeists you hear

about, typically around Halloween? Late October is the one time of the year when a lot of stories suddenly surface in the media about ghosts and goblins. FYI: To my knowledge, though I thought they were wonderfully creepy in the *Harry Potter* books, there is no such thing as a goblin. There are many horrors waiting to be discovered between living monsters and the dead (but not quite gone) but you can scratch goblins off your list of things to be terrified about.

Anyway, each October the media report all the occult stories they ignore the rest of the year. Make no mistake: those scary and weird stories you only hear about around Halloween are going on throughout the year, everywhere, all the time. Haunted houses are big with media and loom large in our imaginations. There's at least one house in every town everyone knows is haunted. There's a lot more than one, actually. Those reporters giggling about the plight of the trapped dead have no idea how many haunted houses there really are.

Lesson 23 A: if you don't want to live in a haunted house, get the ground blessed, build new and not over an old Indian burial ground. If a contractor doesn't have a heart attack on the premises while he's hammering nails or putting in the wiring, you're probably fine, at least for a while.

Lesson 23 B: if you don't want to live in a haunted house, don't die in your house.

Many states require that realtors disclose to potential buyers a house was a murder scene. What people don't know is that some states require full disclosure if the house for sale is haunted, as well. That's for real. Isn't it crazy that the rest of the year we act like paranormal, supernormal or supernatural stuff — whatever you want to call it — is only for loony people with no life skills trying to sell you something?

Remember Lesson 13? Denial. Civilization lives and breathes as it does because of the power of denial. No one can explain ghostly phenomena, but anyone, even your closest friends and family, will be eager to try to explain it away. Reality is too scary.

Lesson 24: sometimes you won't be able to tell the difference between what's accepted as common reality and the Unseen. You'll worry that you really are crazy. You aren't, so don't let that worry drive you insane.

Radio waves were always with us. The burst of the Big Bang left radio static that washes over earth forever. While cave people wandered around chasing food and tried to figure out fire, radio waves were filling the air. Somebody had to build a radio receiver to catch that static for the first time.

That's what the Unseen is. Someday we'll figure out a lens to look through so anybody and everybody can see the world as you and I do. (I'm assuming that, if you're reading this, you probably already see the dead. If not, you can continue to pretend it's a work of fiction if that makes you feel better.)

Or perhaps you're waiting for some kind of lens to be built so you'll see the dead, too. Then this book will be more useful to you as a manual. (Things are much more twisted than simply worrying about the dead wandering around, but I'll get to that soon.)

When you can see the Unseen, you'll want to look away. There are good reasons why the Powers That Be do not want everybody reminded how close death is all the time.

The Powers That Be also have terrible reasons to hide the truth from us.

Lesson 25: No matter what, everyone afflicted with the sight thinks it's the worst thing that could ever happen to them. You'd have to be a maniac to think seeing the dead every day everywhere is a happy thing. There's too much sadness and yearning among the dead. They aren't optimistic about the future because all they're really doing is looking at the past. If you like seeing all that naked need too much, get help. There's an excellent chance you're a killer robot sociopath.

On the other hand, over time and as you get used to it, it's not *all* bad, either. What first feels like a terrible curse may eventually soften to a rotten annoyance (if you study these lessons and apply them.) You may even change enough to look on your power as a gift. Probably not, but maybe.

Or maybe I'm just a killer robot sociopath.

# 9

**I** awoke as the train rolled into New York, headed for
Penn Station. I was as excited and nervous as you'd expect
so I texted Mama to let her know her little girl was about
to step off the train in the Big Apple. You can always tell
when a rube hits NYC. They're always looking up and
they call it, "The Big Apple." I was no exception.

I wasn't prepared for the crush of people. Anywhere in
Iowa, if you want to go somewhere, you can do it by
walking in a straight line. You can stroll as slowly as you
like. In New York, the sidewalk is for brisk paces and
weaving around people. I was weaving around people, the
living and the dead.

We've already covered ignoring them. Conveniently,
that's what you're supposed to do with *live* people in the
city, too. In small towns across America, the locals will
think you're stuck up if you don't smile and say hello as
you meet. In really small towns like Medicament, it's bad
manners to refuse to wave at passing cars. In NYC, ghost
or not, avoid eye contact. The fear is the living will ask you
for money or hit on you. The dead might tell you their life

stories. Sometimes they have a problem they expect you to fix. Mostly they just stare, hoping for a sympathetic eye. Sometimes they follow you home.

I fell into seeing ghosts. I wasn't on some kind of quest. I fixed Petra's problem because I didn't have a choice. What happened at Shibboleth wasn't heroics. I was just trying to avoid being another of Moorely's victims.

The job of ghost detective doesn't pay so it's more of a hobby than a part-time job.

But what happens if you fail to avoid a ghost? At some point, by accident or on purpose, you're going to walk through one. Lesson 26 is about personal boundaries: keep your shields up and avoid close contact if you can.

My first time was by accident. I bumped into a couple of people in my first few minutes in New York. I didn't know the rhythm of city sidewalks yet. I was used to more space around me. Around Penn Station, at least, people are always in a hurry, squeezing between others and, failing that, sometimes even shouldering people aside.

I got shoved into somebody. Or, rather, *through* somebody. He was a large African American man looking down the street, hand raised, trying to hail a cab. I didn't get what happened at first. I just felt cold. The words, "bone chill" come to mind.

Stumbling through a person is, as you might expect, surprising. It's also confusing and, for a moment, I felt a stab of a headache. My stomach felt bloated and I had pain over my kidneys as if someone punched me there with two heavy fists. I stopped breathing for a moment. As soon as I was on the other side of the big man, I coughed and sputtered and spit.

I looked up at him. He smiled down at me. Then he

stepped into the street and threw himself in front of a speeding cab.

I shrieked but the cab moved on. The driver remained oblivious and undisturbed. The streaming crowd spared me a look of surprise and annoyance. I won't say shock. Nothing seems to shock New Yorkers. When they encounter anything horrific or unnatural, they tend to shrug and say, "It's New York. Anything can happen here." And it does.

I blinked and the big man was standing at the curb again. He looked at me and smiled wider. I stood there shaking and listened to my pulse pound in my ears as he peered down the street. Then he threw himself in front of the next cab that drove past.

Some suicides are just sad people hoping for an audience. I was annoyed with the man's exhibitionism at first. Then, as I rubbed my kidneys and gritted my teeth against the last throb of the headache, I realized he'd been a dying man in a lot of pain. His name was Johnny. I'd received a quick pulse of the disease he had endured every day and night. No wonder he killed himself. And now, for some reason I could not fathom, he seemed condemned to repeat his suicide as fast as New York could supply Yellow Cabs.

For ten bucks, I once asked a medium on Coney Island for her take on the ghosts of suicide. (Be careful whom you tell the truth to, for obvious reasons. See Lessons 1 through 4. There are other reasons not to ask, too. See below.)

Mistress Sasha (not Mr. Chang's daughter Sasha) was an older woman who worked as a Coney Island medium. She informed me that, in her spiritualist tradition, "suicide is an affront to God." She told me in confident tones that the successful suicide is condemned to spend the rest of the time that would have been their lifespan, "awake and regretting their choice." Mistress Sasha said. " Life is a gift. Reject a gift from God at your peril."

My gaze lingered over the scooped gold lame dress that pushed her boobs up and out. Across that shelf of flesh was a display of various crystals and totems, each hanging from a separate necklace. A small, white price tag was attached to each of those necklaces. Several gold chains spilled into the cavern of her cleavage. It occurred to me I was seeking serious advice from someone whose fashion tips would be hideous. "What do you mean by 'awake and regretting?'"

"They get buried," Mistress Sasha said. "Suppose you kill yourself at twenty and you were meant to die at eighty. That's sixty years, rotting in a pine box and thinking about the worms swimming through you before you're allowed to progress to the next evolution."

"The what?"

"Reincarnation. You get to try again."

"After all that torment, why would you want to come back?"

Mistress Sasha shrugged and offered to continue chatting with me for another ten dollars. Since what she had to say didn't reflect anything I'd seen, I thanked her for her time. As I stood to go, she pressed a homemade business card into my hand. One side advertised her clairvoyant services. The other side of the card pushed her dog walking service.

"Call me," Mistress Sasha said. "I'll be your personal suicide hotline, honey. I only charge $2.99 a minute."

I couldn't take Mistress Sasha seriously. Petra had been trapped at the hospital after she committed suicide, but I felt far too close to her to think she deserved any more punishment. As for the man in the street by Penn Station, he'd been in too much pain to deny him relief from suicide. But I don't know why the man who threw himself under the cab did so after death. I can tell you all sorts of things about what to expect when you're alive. But motivations? That's not always clear.

I looked up the neuroscience of motivations once. According to the leading minds in leading minds, no one really knows their true motivation to do anything. If you're hungry, you eat, sure. But what cascade of chemicals leads someone to dream of becoming a quantity surveyor, dermatologist or cost accountant? Motivation needs a capital M for Mystery. Many neuroscientists think everything is, by some process we don't understand, determined before we actually have a cogent thought. Put simply, we do things. It's not logical. It's pre-logical. After we do something, that's when we come up with the rationalization of our choice (if you can call that a choice at all.)

If the neurologists are right, then this life is a play and our roles are already set and there is no free will. We're just actors, reading someone else's lines. That sounds kind of hopeless and lacks room for improvisation and joy, doesn't it?

That's why I decided my motivation is to try to make life and death better for the living and the dead. At least, I think that's my motivation.

Lesson 27: Charlatans are of no help, but science may one day answer all our questions about life and the afterlife. Until then, no scientist will take questions and problems surrounding our ghost world seriously enough to be useful. They just give you a smug laugh and act like dicks about it.

While we're waiting for an intelligent, sincere and better dressed medium to stand up and lead us forward with deeper answers, we'll have to get comfortable with ambiguity.

I threw Madame Sasha's business card away. Lesson 28: Don't trust advice from people who say they can see the future but dress like a billboard for New Age knick knacks. A real medium would get rich off the stock market and betting on the Super Bowl.

Think you're a real medium for the spirit world? To test your skills and sensitivity, go down to Penn Station at the Southeast corner of 33$^{rd}$ and 8$^{th}$. Day or night, Johnny's still there, throwing himself under every Yellow Cab that comes along.

# 10

Lesson 29: Ghosts are often, but not always, tied to a place. Johnny doesn't budge from 33$^{rd}$ and 8$^{th}$, for instance. Petra was stuck in Shibboleth Mental Hospital, apparently incapable of taking a walk outside to enjoy the sights of Mason City, Iowa. Brad stood his watch in Medicament, outside in the grass or under the tree in my backyard. I never once saw him go inside his family's farmhouse.

Ghosts work by rules, but no one really knows what those rules are. Each phantom is an individual. However, it seems that many souls are tied to place by the trauma of death. Therefore, wherever you end up dying, plan carefully, just in case. For instance, I'd choose to be murdered in a place with a nice view. If you go ghost, no one knows how long you're going to stand around, haunting.

If it comes to that, maybe I'll watch the end of the world from the spire of the Freedom Tower or from an observation portal on the International Space Station. It might take some doing to arrange that, of course.

I stayed at the Sumner Hotel for my first few nights in Brooklyn. It was the cheapest deal I could find and it was close to the subway. I thought I'd be lonely, but I kept busy exploring. I did think about Brad a lot. I missed his arms around me. I could only imagine that he missed his arms, too.

For all the time I'd stared back at my dead farm boy boyfriend, he told me nothing. I could feel want and need, but there were no words. Maybe the pain of the want and need eclipsed anything he could say.

Mostly, I wished I could share those first days in New York City with him. It is an amazing place and no one should discover the joys of a strange city alone. I did all the things tourists do to orient myself to my new home, but I did wish he was there so I could share the experience. The City is a hive, and I didn't even really know the Secret City of the Unseen yet.

I took bus tours. I saw the Statue of Liberty and Central Park. I discovered the joys of Shake Shack and walked along the High Line, an abandoned, elevated railway track perfect for people watching. It was also good for ghost watching.

It was on the High Line that I discovered the power of looking vaguely pissed off and bored. Every New Yorker cultivates that look and, after a little practice, I got it down. Unless they're loitering, New Yorkers all walk like they are late for an appointment. In Iowa, people don't hurry on escalators. New Yorkers don't have time to ride escalators. They keep moving and they climb.

I needed to practice looking like a native citizen. I was a little nervous being on my own in the big city for the first time, sure, but the dead worried me more than the panhandlers. In the West Village, I saw a woman in a bonnet and long skirts pushing a fancy blue baby stroller. It was so big and fancy, *stroller* wasn't the right word. Judging by her style of dress, I guessed she'd have called it a baby carriage or a pram.

The misty wistfuls in period dress look a little more wispy than the fresher ghosts. It's as if they are deaf people who have been deaf so long, they're forgetting the language of living. They seem to have lost how life feels. When I spotted the woman with the pram, I hoped at first that there was some kind of cosplay convention nearby. As she drew nearer, I couldn't help myself. I glanced in the pram. Mercifully, it was empty.

When I looked up, the woman looked at me sharply. I looked at the screen of my phone and adjusted my headphones. I turned up Taylor Swift's *Blank Space* and busied myself looking for a Beyonce track. When I raised my head again, the woman had pulled back her bonnet to reveal half her head was burned to her naked, black scalp. I tried to keep my face impassive and jogged away. I ran a few blocks before I dared to look back. To my relief, the woman in the long black dress was not running after me, pushing an empty baby carriage.

During those early days in New York City, I started each day at dawn. I walked the city and ranged farther and farther afield using the subway. Everywhere I went, men called after me. Some were polite and their friendliness seemed as open as the usual good morning wishes I would expect in small town Iowa. Others seemed more aggressive. "Hey, baby! You're looking good today! What's your name?" I gave them a stone faced nod and quickened my pace — *hi, ho Silver! Away!* — *who was that masked girl?*

The stares and catcalls came in a steady stream. Not just for me, of course, but for many women. Only the elderly seemed to disappear into the camouflage of age. After a while, I tried to think of the barrage as part of the noise of the street, blending with the cacophony of engines and horns and the march of millions slowly pounding the sidewalk to concrete dust.

Not long before my pilgrimage to the big city, I would not have taken all the attention with such stoicism. However, I'd discovered once you've had a hand in — er...a *knee* in — castrating a sexual predator? Let's just say it's empowering.

I fell in love with New York, despite the dead and the catcalls. New York City feels like it's alive and humming at the center of the universe. There is something in the air there besides pollution. The city is made for the young and ambitious with hope in their hearts and an unshakeable and stupid belief in their unquestioned potential.

I had good dreams in Iowa: love, safety, hot wood stoves on cold nights, room for puppies to roam and all the coziness of a life that would unfold as I predicted. In New York, I dreamt new dreams. I was going to divine the mysteries of the Secret City that boils beneath the Seen. I'd make the Unseen my bitch. I wasn't sure how to do that, but seeing what others did not made me feel special, like whoever was writing my role had decided to create something different and fun.

My first New York City nights might have been lonely if I'd been awake. However, since each day was a long hike, by nightfall I was back at the Sumner, exhausted and ready to sleep until the sun returned.

After a week at the hotel, I started to form a plan. I needed a place to live. If I stayed at any hotel, my money would run out quickly and I wanted to make it last as long as possible. If I went back to Medicament I'd feel like a failure. Also, if the lady with the pram from the 1800s was any indication, my zombie boyfriend in waiting might have more patience than I had life left.

I had my father's last known address but I didn't want to show up on his doorstep. There was a better than even chance he didn't live there anymore. Either way, I didn't want to show up looking like I wanted help or a stretch of floor space to sleep on. I wanted to make my appearance in his life look more casual. Like, "Hey, yeah, so I live in New York now and I just thought I'd keep in touch since we're family and all." I'd been through too much to play the part of the estranged hick daughter in the big city, even if that's really what I was.

Mama raised me to believe your parents are the people who raise you, not just some random biological accident of birth. When I was little, each Christmas I'd ask Mama where Daddy was. Her eyes would get wet and she'd shrug and say, "Anybody can be a father, but you have no Daddy. He opted out."

By my sixth Christmas, I understood that I shouldn't ask anymore. At nineteen, I can say the move East wasn't just about tracking down my father. I was curious, naturally, but I needed the city for something else besides an escape from Medicament and my armless sentinel.

I came with a more mundane goal, too. Just like millions of others who come to New York, I wanted to lose myself in the city in the hope that, someday, the city would pause a moment and say, "That's the famous Tamara Smythe. She's a big deal. She's one of ours, you know."

Of course, I had no idea how to get that famous and successful. I thought, as everyone who comes to New York City thinks, that it would all work out somehow. It's a magical place, figuratively and literally. It makes you think you can do anything and you're too cool to fail.

Sorry. I didn't know it at the time but, despite all my good grades and trying hard, I was an idiot.

# 11

I needed to learn more about the dead. Cities have more
live people, therefore they have more dead people. I didn't
know where my life was going, but I needed a target-rich
environment to figure out what was going on. Ultimately, I
needed to figure a way to lift the curse. I guessed that it
had happened to me for some reason. Once I discovered
that reason and did whatever I needed to do, I hoped to
be able to let the hauntings disappear. I'd somehow find a
way not to see Brad in the field when I went back to
Medicament. Failing that, I'd find a way to allow him to
move on or find peace — whatever we are all supposed to
do once we lose the knack for breathing.

But first, I needed somewhere to live so I wasn't a
tourist anymore. I looked through online listings but
everything looked too expensive to me. I was used to Iowa
prices. New York City rents looked like the mortgage
payment for a mansion back home.

"You are home," I reminded myself. I'd thought I was
going to marry Brad Evers and live happily ever after.
After a brief courtship, I knew my second choice was to

marry New York City.

I didn't know how long it would take me to get a job, but my first order of business was to find a bachelor apartment (a bachelorette, I guess.) It's difficult searching for a job when you don't have a permanent address. It's also hard to find an apartment when you don't have a job.

Rent control apartments in New York are only passed down through families, so I had to find a rent-stabilized apartment. Cheaper apartments are so hard to come by, no one wants to leave them. When they do become available, landlords don't need to advertise. The people who find these rare gems are well-connected with a vast network of friends to tip them off. Of course, I knew no one.

The dead gave me an idea of how I'd find an apartment, though. Since this will work in any city, let's call this Lesson 30: Download an app to your phone with an Emergency Services scanner and get ready to run to the apartments of the recently departed. Dead people vacate apartments, (or at least technically they are *supposed* to leave.)

When an ambulance calls in a 10-83, that's a dead body. When the fire department radios in a 10-45, Code 1, that's a dead body, too. Make a note of the address and keep your sneakers on because you're in a race to get there before the apartment is snatched up by someone else.

As ambulances or the Coroner pulled away from apartment after apartment, I'd just happen to show up at the landlord's door asking about any vacancies, eager to fill out an application and ready to ante up a security deposit and first and last month's rent.

"Well," they'd say, "one of our elderly residents just

died in her apartment. Does that bother you?"

"Let me see it first and I'll let you know."

It still took me almost a month to find a small studio apartment on Church Avenue in Flatbush. I loved that I lived in a place called Flatbush, but it wasn't located in the best place for someone like me. I was to live smack between the Downstate Medical Center and the massive Holy Cross Cemetery. In other words, I moved into Dead Central. I didn't know that when I took the apartment. Seeing the misty wistfuls wander and pace and wait throughout the city is a shock. I wanted a target-rich environment and, boy, did I find it.

Moving from small town Iowa to New York was a culture shock, too. The building was a walk-up above a block of stores unlike anything in Medicament. A barber shop sat on one corner next to a secondhand store that advertised books, watches and necklaces. Next was Chouchounette, a boutique filled with designer clothes, handmade jewelry and handbags. Next to that was a store that sold African movies and the last store on the ground floor advertised African hair braiding. A Jerk City stood on the corner, but it was closed up and graffiti covered the metal security gate at the restaurant's entrance.

My apartment was on the third floor. Even with every piece of furniture hauled away, the place smelled like old lady lavender. However, the old lady had kept the place spotless. She was also dead and gone and apparently had the good manners not to be too attached to the place.

I bought myself a sleeping bag and a hot plate and a small pot. My first meal in my own apartment was a cup of instant chicken noodle soup and instant hot chocolate. Dinner came from envelopes, but it was all mine.

I texted Mama: *1ˢᵗ nite in my new apt! So cool!*

Mama had the grace not to remind me I could come home any time I wanted. She didn't say, "Or we could move to the next town. I can commute to work at the drugstore."

She held back on suggesting, "Maybe Northwestern could still cancel your deferment. You could start back at your studies right away without dropping a stitch!"

Not that night she didn't, anyway, so you can see why I love Mama.

The hardwood floor wasn't comfortable and I'd forgotten to buy a pillow so I shoved my backpack underneath my head. I missed my soft bed back at the Sumner Hotel, but I lay awake most of that first night listening to the traffic and thinking how crazy it was that I was in New York, nineteen and alone.

But I was doing it!

I think that first night was probably the second time in my life I'd really felt like a grown, adult woman.

The first time was with Brad after we made love. It was Christmas night in his parents' basement. (I couldn't wait for the summer grass to grow tall. That was a good hiding place for us, but it was months away and I was eager.)

I can still picture Brad, naked and unselfconscious, reclined on the rug in front of the family Christmas tree. I covered up, wrapping myself in a blanket.

Mr. Evers had grown that Christmas tree. When it was ready, he and Brad and Chad cut the tree down while Mrs. Evers and I stayed by the fire and strung popcorn into garlands with a needle and thread. Brad's Mom told me that decorating the Christmas tree with popped corn was an Evers family tradition. "Is that corny?" she asked.

"Not until you said that, it wasn't," I said. "It was sweet."

Mrs. Evers smiled and watched my face as she told me, "I hope you continue this tradition, Tammy, with your own children. With my grandchildren."

As soon as his family was out of the house, Brad and I saw our chance to play house. I'll never forget the first time. No one does. It was chilly in the room and the Evers family were out visiting with friends. Despite the cold, I was still warm all over.

Afterward, Brad gave me his dimpled smile and said, "So…we've lost our virginity."

"I didn't lose mine," I told him. "I chucked it at you. I know exactly where it went."

"We're good together," he said.

"I'm not sure. I think we should practice. A lot."

He chuckled and nodded and stared at me.

"As long as I've known you," I said, "I've never seen you have a moment of self-doubt. How did you get so confident?"

He shrugged. "Born with it. Some people have to settle for brains. I've got luck and self-confidence. That'll do." He winked and looked down at himself. "Besides, I'm not really self-confident. I'm cocky! Look! It's happening again!"

I thought about that night and how perfect the future looked for us. That is, until Brad's good luck turned bad.

Alone in a tiny, bare apartment and thinking of Brad, I suddenly felt like being a young independent woman with no plans kind of sucked.

*Brad and Tam. Tam and Brad. The forever couple.*

I thought of Brad's arms and how it must have hurt

him to have his limbs ripped from his body and chewed up with metal teeth. And still, despite his mortal wounds, Brad called me, hoping to hear my voice before he collapsed to the floor. Instead, he bled to death on the rug his mother bought in a bazaar in Egypt.

Now I wasn't part of the forever couple. I was just Tam. Alone and not near as brave as I tried to look. I waited a long time, trying to hold back the flood, but tears do have their way, don't they?

# 12

Lesson 31: If you can see the dead, you are not alone.

My little apartment on Church Avenue was bare, but that hardly mattered since all I did was sleep there. Each day I went out in search of a job. I'd printed off resumes that looked too short, no matter how creative I got with white space and a large font. Besides working for Mama, being a camp counselor and babysitting, I was short on job experience. I'd planned my extracurricular activities in high school around looking good to a university admissions committee, not a boss. I didn't see how I could monetize a black belt in Hapkido. If I'd studied jazz piano instead of classical, maybe I could have played in a hotel bar or something.

Though I had worked for Mama in the drugstore stocking shelves, I hadn't even worked the cash register. I wasn't qualified to be a pharmacy assistant, of course, so my first thought was I could get a job as a waitress. It's the new girl in the big city cliche, but getting that gig turned out to be harder than it looked.

The nicer restaurants weren't hiring. Several store

managers noted that I hadn't even worked at a McDonald's, so how did I think I'd fare managing a whole section when their restaurant was busy?

I kept running into the same brick walls:

"We require experience. We don't give experience."

"Come back after you've worked in fast food for a couple of years, kid."

"We serve alcohol so you're not even old enough to work here."

I would have taken any job in food service, but the combined cash and tip minimum wage rate was eight dollars an hour. I didn't want to burn through my settlement from Shibboleth so I kept looking.

I looked at want ads and scrolled through ads on Craigslist. I knew I was getting desperate when I began to consider the creepier ads:

"Female and male models needed, Rubenesque preferred. Must *love* ice popsicles and/or day-long lollipops. Generous compensation."

"Crimefighter requires sidekick. You supply powers and cape. I supply a logo (to be emblazoned across your chest and cape) that matches my own brand. Fighting skills required to subdue evildoers. Sewing skills a plus."

"No experience required as long as you are a Cat Whisperer! Our kitties don't like baths and we need a motivated expert in cat wrangling to keep our army of angry cats clean! Save us from being a couple of old cat ladies on *Hoarders*! Compensation to be discussed. Job perk!: Cuddling and purring at the end of each day!"

I looked at that last one a long time. The fact that, "Compensation to be discussed," was the only line that ended in a period instead of an exclamation point did not seem to bode well for my earning potential.

It was a late afternoon at the end of my second week of the job search when I hit my All is Lost moment. I could live on ramen noodles to stretch my budget, but I didn't see how to live in the city without splitting the rent. To make my nest egg last, I'd have to cram four roommates into my tiny apartment.

I'd been walking all day in uncomfortable shoes. I was sweating through a white blouse and trying to look stylish while hiking the city on the job hunt. It was the first week of October and surprisingly hot. My feet hurt and I was thinking about checking out the Cat Whisperer job.

That's when I wandered into Holy Cross Cemetery to find a bench and reevaluate my job search strategy. I had avoided the cemeteries until then, but I needed to sit and rest and, frankly, I was curious what I'd find there. I had pictured an army of the dead, the rotting corpses standing at attention by their headstones, swaying gently in the wind and waiting, mostly in vain, to catch up on the latest family news from those who had survived them.

That sounded like something out of a horror movie. The truth was a little more boring, but creepy. Contrary to what I had expected, the cemetery itself was serene. The real action was outside each gate to the cemetery.

Ghosts of all shapes and sizes and ages took a space along the fence. Their clothes were from various ages I recognized and several I did not. If bell bottom jeans were a capital offense (as they should be) some of the dead might have been executed by the fashion police in the '70s.

I saw several naked men and women stand watch. The naked ones had visible wounds that looked fresh. I looked away and hurried on. When I glanced back, I saw that they paid me no attention. It was as if the dead expected something momentous to happen inside the cemetery at any moment. They stared inward, longingly, at the graves.

After scooting past several of the dead at the West gate, I wandered deeper into Holy Cross. A funeral was taking place and I saw a clutch of people in dark suits and dresses staring at a casket as a priest spoke.

I spotted a green bench, but I almost walked by it. At first, I thought it was occupied by a ghost citizen. An old man in a dark suit stared at the interment proceedings. He was so still that, at a glance, I wasn't sure if he was alive or dead. Then I heard the old guy's cough and wheeze. He didn't sound dead to me, but his wheeze and age suggested he wouldn't have long to wait.

I gave him a nod and sat at the other end of the bench, as far away as possible.

"Good afternoon," he said. He gestured toward the interment, "Good for us...not so good for them, I suppose."

"I suppose," I said.

"Visiting anyone in particular?" he asked.

"No. Just passing through. I'm on the hunt for a job and needed to rest."

"Oh? How's it going?"

"It seems I don't have enough experience to get experience," I said, and immediately regretted it.

Mama always said that the correct answer to, "How are you?" is always, "Fine, thank you."

"Tell 'em you're fine even if your dog's run away and you've pooped your pants 'cuz you're gut shot," Mama said. "Nobody likes a whiner, Tammy girl."

I knew I shouldn't complain to a stranger so I tried to work my way back to sounding cheerful. "I've got some feelers out, though. I'm sure a decent job will pop up soon. In the meantime, this place is a nice break from handing out resumes and dekeing around people all day on the street. Sometimes I weave through the crowd on the sidewalk so much it feels like I'm playing football, or I'm trying to avoid crashing into somebody who's trying to crash into me."

"I understand," he said.

"Sorry. I'm a chatterbox today." Then it occurred to me why I couldn't seem to shut up. I hadn't had a casual conversation with another human being since I'd come to New York. When people are too friendly and open in the city, it's always a cue to be wary.

"It is a beautiful day," the man said, finally. "You'd never believe it is October. So many of the leaves are still clinging to the trees. I love autumn. As the leaves fall, it is as if the maples are raining a gentle fire upon us, reminding us that even the most fleeting of seasons can compensate for brevity with deathly beauty. The leaves are lifeless, but what is better than the dry crunch of colorful leaves under your feet and the smell of the fall reminding us how good it is to be alive?"

"That's very poetic."

He smiled. "I'd have preferred to be a poet. Poetry is easier on the back, but it doesn't pay." He chuckled and turned to give me his full attention. "I talk too much, too. My wife always said I was too familiar with strangers, but that's why I have so many friends."

"That's a good way to be. I come from a small town. I understand. It's weird when everybody knows everybody, too. They all know each other's business."

"That's the joy of the big city," he said. "You can choose who knows you and who doesn't. In a way, that's friendlier, isn't it?"

"Yes. I see what you mean. In a small town, friendly is forced upon you. Here, you can pick your friends. I take it you're friendly with lots of people, though."

The old man smiled. "Precisely what I told my wife. Gregarious is a good way to be. Being guarded at all times is so exhausting." He offered his hand. "My name is Victor. Victor Fuentes."

"Nice to meet you, Mr. Fuentes."

"Please, call me Victor."

"Victor, then. I'm Tamara." We shook hands. "Are you…um…visiting your wife?"

He laughed. "No. My wife — Cynthia — is still alive, sadly. Ex-wife now. We divorced a few years ago and I never got over it. I understand she has a new swain on the Upper East Side." He pointed vaguely beyond the interment ceremony. "She and I still have a plot over there somewhere, ready and waiting. Once she dies, I expect she'll want to be laid to rest there. Then I'll know for certain where to find her."

"Ah," I said. "Isn't it weird? I mean…reserving the plot of ground where…you know…sorry, sir."

"Not at all. It would be very strange if I were your age. At your age, I was immortal. We are all so sure of immortality when we are young and healthy. At my age, you begin to get used to the idea and, at the end of life, I've heard from several close friends that we may even look forward to lying down. So many resist Death who would not think of resisting a nap. It's all the same. Death is a deeper sleep. And this," he gestured to our surroundings, "is one of the most peaceful places in the city. People love Central Park, but there are too many people there for my taste. No matter what the weather, I always take a stroll to Holy Cross. It's my siesta."

He pointed at the cemetery's perimeter in the distance and his lip curled with disdain. "It is such a relief to get away from the hoi polloi."

I straightened in my seat. Something about the curl of his lip told me he wasn't only talking about the crush of the busy sidewalks and the push of constant traffic that formed the city's pulse. "The hoi polloi?"

He glanced my way. "The masses. They are always there. They're waiting."

I wasn't sure what I could say. I had to be careful not to sound crazy in case I was wrong. "These…hoi polloi…are they a reminder? Like fallen leaves? Is that what the hoi polloi are?"

He fixed me with a steady gaze. "A reminder. Yes. Time is short for us, is that not true?"

"But sometimes, for the masses, they have lots of time, don't they? Just to stand around and stare. Deathly stares." I felt like we were sparring partners in the first round, throwing a few feints and ready to retreat, feeling each other out.

Victor crossed one knee over the other, adjusted the crease of his dress pants fussily and picked off a bit of lint. "Tamara, was it?"

"Tamara Smythe."

"Lovely. Tamara, did you know that in ancient times, people called ghosts, 'shades'? Later on, ghosts were called phantasms. Isn't that a wonderful word?"

"Phantasms? Yes. I hadn't heard that one. I like it a lot. Specters is a cool word, too."

He smiled and I could see the handsome young man he'd once been. His eyes were large and sharp and I thought of a bird of prey. He missed nothing. I could sense where he was going. It was then I realized I'd been very tense for a long time and now I could relax.

"There's a problem with the word phantasms, though," he said. Victor watched my face carefully to see how I'd react.

"What's that, sir?"

"It's too much like the word phantasmagorical. It suggests that phantasms aren't real."

"It does seem to suggest that, doesn't it?"

"Do you believe in ghosts, Miss Tamara Smythe?"

"You know I do."

"How do you know?"

"You know how. Because I had to walk by a bunch at the gate and they're lined up along the fence, all around this cemetery. They look like they want in."

Victor gave me a slow nod and reached out. I took his hand and we shook again, slowly and solemnly. "Welcome to the club, Miss Smythe."

# 13

Lesson 32: The first rule of Ghost Club is the same as the first rule of *Fight Club*. Shut up about Ghost Club. At least, don't talk to people who aren't in the club. If you do, they'll likely put you in a mental hospital. And who knows what terrible things might come of that? Yeah, put your hands down. That question was rhetorical and won't be on the test.

*(You will be tested, though. We are all tested.)*

Lesson 33: When you do find a kindred spirit who sees spirits, spill your guts and share experiences because otherwise it's a great, lonely world.

I asked Victor Fuentes how he started seeing ghosts. He told me he owned an antique shop in Park Slope. "The dead have a lot of treasures they want to hold on to. The people who die but don't go are a nostalgic lot. When I started in this business I was thirteen, moving old furniture for my father. I'd ride around in the truck and we'd go to auctions, mostly estate sales. Sometimes we'd go straight to a house to see what they had to sell. Then we'd take a dresser or a commode or something back to the shop. If a piece of furniture was constructed of a nice wood, I'd strip it down to the original and give it a fresh varnish. My eyes watered and my hands would burn from the chemicals we used to strip the wood, but there's something special about peeling back the layers to find the secrets underneath, isn't there? We'd spruce up old furniture, sand it smooth and resell it for a little profit. My father had a good eye for a bargain he could mark up heavily.

"One day, I went out on a run with my father to a house in Hoboken. My father haggled with this little old man over the price of a rocker. When they arrived at a price, they shook hands and my father handed the old man a few bills. He told me to put the rocking chair in the back of the truck. I said, 'I can't,' and my father says, 'You can manage it alone. Just be careful going down the stairs so you don't scratch the walls. And I say, 'No. I can't carry it away with the lady still sitting in it. She doesn't want me to take it."

"Only there was no lady in the chair, was there?"

"Not that my father and the widower could see," Victor said.

"Did your father try to get you locked up?"

Victor shook his head. "This was many years ago and my father was old school from the old country. We are in scientific times now, but when I was a boy we had more respect for manifestations of the ineffable."

"What did you do about the chair?"

"Left it. My father looked at me and said, 'You're sure the lady doesn't want us to take the rocking chair?' I said I was sure and we got out of there. The old man chased us out to the truck trying to get us to take her rocking chair. My father didn't even want his money back. The old man planned to remarry. I told him he could remarry, but as long as he had that rocking chair, his dead wife would always be in his house and watching."

"Watching him or watching *over* him?"

"Not sure. When you think about it, either way is kind of ominous, isn't it? As a man who has been happily married and happily divorced, I can tell you it's somewhat off-putting to think a former lover can decide unilaterally that they will be part of your life forever, no matter what."

I felt a pang in my stomach about Brad then. The pain was mixed with guilt. I had conceded that my poor farm boy boyfriend could have Medicament, Iowa. Every night I pictured his ghost out in the field under a cold rain or cool moonlight, waiting for a glimpse of me. It was selfish of him not to move on after his arms got ripped off. It was selfish of me to run away.

"Where are they supposed to go?" I asked.

"Heaven, maybe. At least, that's what my grandmother told me. She had the sight, as well. She thought those who die in a state of grace but are not yet pure enough to rise to heaven. The impure dead must endure the temporary torment of the half-life, between worlds. I guess that means we're in Purgatory, too, since we can see their torment. They say Florida is God's waiting room, but I've traveled the Earth. They're everywhere and they're all waiting for something."

"You don't sound sure about the Heaven thing."

"I'm not. I think my grandmother was guessing, too. But hers was a developed gift. She not only saw the dead, she saw what was wrong with the living. She told my father he should stop smoking cigarettes or he would die of lung cancer."

87

"What happened?"

"He didn't stop. He died of lung cancer."

"That's true of lots of people who smoke, though."

"I would agree, Tamara, but my grandmother told my father to go to the doctor before it was too late. She said there was something in his left lung. He was afraid to go to the doctor and, by the time he did, it was too late. The X-rays showed a big spot on his lung. Soon he was spitting up blood."

Victor pointed in the same direction he had before, beyond the funeral ceremony. "My father's ashes are buried over there in the family plot. I hope my ex-wife gets lost at sea or something because if she gets buried next to my father, he'll be furious." He chuckled and shook his head. "Dad always hated Cynthia. He wasn't all wrong."

"I'm sorry for your loss."

Victor shrugged. "Everyone dies of something eventually. At least my father had the grace to die and go. He didn't decide to hang out and frown at me every time I make a bad deal on a chest of drawers and a dish set."

"Are there many others?" I asked. "Like us, I mean?"

His lips went thin. "There are more than will admit the truth. It goes deep. The Powers That Be know, I'm sure. How could they not? No doubt someone is in a lab somewhere at this moment working on the mystery."

"Trying to send the ghosts on?"

He laughed. "Trying to weaponize the dead."

I shuddered. "Please. Don't. I've already seen too many zombie movies. This is too much like that. A bunch of those people, when they died, they look pretty much chewed up."

"And that's not pretty."

"No." I saw Brad again, standing in the field behind his house. I imagined how hard it must have been for him to kick in the front door to get to the phone. He should have called 911 and tried to make it for the road. Maybe the extra few minutes would have made the difference between life and a living death. Maybe someone in a passing car could have…nah, probably not.

Victor checked his watch and stood. He reached to the side of the bench and, when he straightened, the old man held a straight cane topped with an ornate handle of silver and gold. "I'm so sorry. I must get back to the shop. My siesta time is over and I'm expecting a buyer."

He tucked the cane under his arm and pulled a shiny case from an inside pocket. The case held business cards. He extracted one card and the case disappeared back into his suit pocket.

I held out my hand for the card but he held up a finger to tell me to wait. "Tamara, how old are you, if I may?"

"Almost twenty."

"Mm-hm. And do you possess a valid driver's license?"

"Yes."

"Are you a good driver?"

"Started on a friend's tractor. I've driven deliveries since I was sixteen for my mom's drugstore."

He pulled a short calligraphic pen from his shirt pocket, unscrewed the top and wrote on the back of the card. A moment later he offered it to me.

"Call the number on the front of the card if you want to go deeper, Tamara. Or you can find me here every day, for that matter. There is more to this than you know."

We shook hands and I watched him go. For an old man, he seemed to manage to slip through the crowd of the watching dead with ease and avoided touching them. Victor didn't seem to need the cane at all.

As he stepped to the curb, a large man in a long coat and a three-piece suit (an ensemble that looked far too hot for the weather) waited for Victor. The man was built strong and top heavy, like he spent all his spare time working his chest and arms but never his legs. The man's nose was pushed to one side and he had cauliflower ears. Back in Iowa, we called guys like that hard rocks.

The man walked quickly toward Victor and said something I couldn't hear. I headed for the street and reached for my phone, ready to call the police for my new friend. I slowed when I saw the old man put a hand on the hard rock's arm and they threw their heads back in a shared laugh.

A moment later, the big man gave a slight bow and opened the back door of a long white limousine sitting at the curb. Victor climbed in the back and soon they drove away.

I looked at the business card in my hand. The lettering on the front was a raised gold script that read: Victor Fuentes, Collector and Broker. Exclusive Antiques and Rare Art for the Discerning Eye.

On the rear of the card I found Victor's short note in a slightly slanted script. If I hadn't seen him write it out, I might have suspected his perfect penmanship had been produced by a machine. Below a telephone number, his note read: *Tomorrow morning, please call Sam about a position that will suit your unique talents.* ~ *V.*

It seemed I'd made my first friend in New York.

Lesson 34: You'll avoid a ton of trouble if you don't speak to strange men in parks.

# 14

Sam turned out to be a woman. She answered my call with a crisp, "You've reached Castille. Samantha Biggs speaking. How may I help you?"

When I began to explain how I got her number, she said, "Oh, yes. Victor's girl in the cemetery. Fitting. Do you have a suit? You're going to need a suit. Pinstripes are fine, checks are not. Not black, navy blue. We find blue makes our people more approachable. I can see you tomorrow for orientation. Can you have a suit by then?"

"I don't know what the job is yet."

She laughed. "Victor likes to be mysterious and I so hate to spoil his fun. I'll tell you up front, it's nothing illegal. Mostly the job is driving and meeting people, though if you'd like to expand your duties in the future, we can discuss that as we go. Are you a good driver?"

"Yes. I've never been in an accident." That was true, though it might have something to do with the fact that I never drove much. When I did drive, it was in Iowa. Most roads are so flat and wide and straight, it's like driving on an airport runway.

"Do you know the city well?" she asked.

"Yes," I lied. I figured as long as I had my phone, GPS could talk me through New York City's labyrinth.

"Good. Report at nine sharp. Oh, and wear toe caps."

"Toe caps? I don't — "

"I mean no open toed shoes. We don't show off our piggies on the job. No sandals and low heels are best."

"Should I be getting the job before I have an interview?" I asked.

She paused and took a breath. I could sense her smile through the phone. "You've already been interviewed, sweetie. If Victor says hire you, I hire you. I manage things but Victor owns the place."

"So I'll be delivering antiques?"

"Often, yes." She laughed and I started to get irritated at the game that was being played on me. I almost hung up, but Samantha quickly reassured me. "I'm not laughing at you, dear. It's Victor. He's as wily as he is charming. Antiques is one of Victor's business interests. The big money is in funeral services. You'll be working for Castille Funeral Services."

"Oh," I said.

"Still interested?"

"How much does it pay?"

"Not as much as you'd think, but not bad. I can guarantee you'll pay off the suit quickly if you don't go too crazy with your credit card."

I had one of Mama's credit cards for emergencies, but I was determined not to use it.

"We can discuss those details tomorrow and I'll have some tax paperwork for you to sign and whatnot. Are you still interested now?"

I'd been looking for a job steadily and I couldn't seem to break into a decent entry-level position. "Yes," I said finally.

It's startling what our choices can add up to. I was soon to learn how deep and dark and twisted the paths of the Secret City really are. A yes? A no? It's like we're all running blind and we only see the path we took when we look back at the end of the journey.

Turn right and you die in a fiery car crash. Turn left and maybe you meet the love of your life by a school water fountain. You make love and you hope, eventually, to make babies together and live happily ever after (though happily ever after only happens if you don't tell a story to the end). Life and death are dice we throw every morning we open our eyes. Maybe it works out pretty well for a while. Lose focus for a moment and maybe your arms get ripped off in a giant piece of farm machinery.

Or worse.

Worse was on its way.

# 15

Castille Funeral Services was a low building at the edge of a cemetery filled with mausoleums. I'd never seen a mausoleum except for pictures of New Orleans.

In Iowa, we tend to bury our dead underground, not above it. I almost said: In Iowa, we bury people, "the right way." But I'd been in New York about a month so I like to think I was getting cosmopolitan and less judgy about alien ways of doing things.

As soon as I entered the funeral home, a gentle chime sounded in the distance. The carpet was thick under my feet and it made me think how my apartment needed a rug. My first priority was to buy a futon since I was still sleeping on the hardwood floor and my sleeping bag was too thin to be comfortable.

A tall, fortyish blonde breezed out of her office. "Good morning, I'm Samantha Biggs. How may I help you?"

"I'm Tamara Smythe. We spoke on th — "

"Good. On time and not too much makeup. My last part-timer used so much hairspray, I'm still recovering."

"Uh. Thanks."

She looked me up and down again, nodded and shook my hand with one firm, perfunctory pump. "The lapels are a little wide, but actually, nice suit."

I looked down at myself and smiled proudly. "I found it at a discount store. I got a good deal on it and the owner altered it for me right away."

Samantha's smile disappeared and I sensed I'd said the wrong thing. My unease didn't disappear when she said, "Given the circumstances, I suppose that was...shrewd."

So much for feeling sophisticated and cosmopolitan. Which made me think Samantha Biggs was a snob and she was going to be a shrew of a boss. Actually, she was a bit of a snob, but she wasn't a shrew. She was just busy. Samantha always moved with purpose and if a conversation began to go off on a personal tangent, she put it back on track by answering a question that had not been asked. She had the edgy energy of someone who is constantly working and harried yet is trying desperately not to look hurried.

"I moved here from Iowa recently," I said.

"This building used to be a school," Samantha said. She beckoned me to follow her. "Victor bought the place in 1989 and renovations took almost a year. We repaint the entire place on the inside every Christmas day. We repaint on the outside every Independence Day. We can handle a funeral of two hundred easily and open up that wall for up to four hundred people. If there is overflow, the other visitation rooms are equipped with video for other attendees, but that's rarely necessary."

The corridors were broad and fresh flowers sat atop marble tables at equal intervals. Someone must have positioned those tables carefully, spacing them using a tape measure.

"How many funerals have you attended, Tamara?"

"One."

"I see. Well, the uninitiated have some funny ideas about what we do."

We walked through double doors made of dark wood and emerged in a narrower hallway I was sure no funeral attendee had ever seen. The floor was tile. The walls were bare white here instead of the soft cream and velvet wall paper I'd noticed at the front.

We turned a corner and Samantha brought me to the doorway of an office to introduce me to the staff. Three large desks sat together in a triangle in the middle of the room. A trio of women faced each other throughout the work day. Two were middle-aged and the third, closest to the window, seemed quite elderly.

Three computer towers sat in the triangular hole in the middle of the arrangement. There was something about the odd desk setup that made me think of the three witches in *Hamlet* at their cauldron. *Bubble, bubble, toil and trouble....*

The women looked pleasant enough, however, and it was impossible for me to forget their names. "We're all named Linda," the first one said as she shook my hand. "One of us is Lynda with a *y*." She pointed to the little old lady peering up at me through circular lenses. "She's the rebel."

Two video screens showed eight security camera angles. "Clyde's at the back door," Lynda said in a voice as thin as paper. "Someone let him in, please."

Samantha stepped to another set of double doors. These were made of steel. In a moment, a large man stepped in and I was introduced to Clyde. His shirt was starched white and pulled tight over his large belly. The white of his shirt emphasized the redness of his cheeks. If we were back at the pharmacy in Medicament, Mama would have told the man to sit at the blood pressure machine for a checkup.

"Tamara is our new part-timer," Samantha told Clyde. "We'll have you show her the ropes on the road next week, I think."

"Yup. Okay." Clyde bobbed his head and Samantha took me by the elbow to point me back up the little hallway. When we'd turned the corner, I'd been looking to the office. I hadn't noticed the two huge steel doors behind me.

"That's the prep room," Samantha said. "We'll save that part of the tour for another day, once you're more acclimated. Now, before we went into the office, what was I saying?"

"You said that the uninitiated have some funny ideas about what you do."

Samantha's eyebrows shot high. Apparently her question had been rhetorical, but she smiled her approval. "Thank you," she said. "I hate to repeat myself. I have a feeling that won't be necessary with you."

"I pick up stuff pretty quickly."

"I'm sure. So here's the deal. When people think of funeral services, they think about the bodies. That's really a small part of it. It's an important part you will be responsible for, but you know what we are?"

I shrugged.

"We are party planners. Subtract the bodies from the equation," she said, "and we could be party planners working any major hotel in the city. A funeral is a prom with one very quiet, very special guest of honor."

I nodded. "As Mama would say, 'Funerals are for the living.'"

Samantha broke into a grin. "*Mama?* Oh my *gawd*, you're for real, aren't you?"

I shrugged again.

"Adorable."

When she caught my annoyed look, she apologized. "Sorry, dear. I was born and raised in Long Island. 'Mama' sounds like someone from a television show."

I didn't want to let her off the hook too easily. Also, as Mama would say, you get a paycheck for your time. If the boss wants your dignity, too, you're getting paid too little and you're in the wrong job. I guess that's Lesson 35, courtesy of Mama.

I cleared my throat. "My mother is from Texas, Miss Biggs. If I say something that sounds like what you've heard off of TV, perhaps it's because in many of the American states you fly over on your vacations, we do, in fact, speak in familiar, friendly colloquialisms and regional idioms. We like it. When you pronounce the *g* in Long Island — as if it's a hard *g* — I can assure you, it sounds very much like a New York cliche, too...but I'm far too polite to say so because," — I smeared Mama's Texas accent on far thicker and heavier that it actually was — "Mama brung me up right. Mama ben to church and she churched me."

Samantha burst out laughing. I thought I was about to go back to hunting for a job in my new secondhand suit. I was wrong.

"It's *Mrs.* Biggs," she said, "but all the staff and my

friends call me Sam. Please call me Sam."

"Sure, Sam."

"We'll start you as a door swinger."

"Okay. A what?"

"You'll greet people at visitations. We serve coffee. We'll need your help doing things like setting out extra chairs. People think all we do is embalming. They have no idea how much we vacuum. We'll give you some time on the inside and you'll attend funerals. After a week, maybe two, Clyde will introduce you to driving the coach. That's what we call the hearse. Three months probation, but if I need to talk to you about something before your probation is up, I'll just tell you straight out. Suppose you're walking around here with your cell phone out during a visitation. I'll tell you right away that's not appropriate."

"Okay."

"Later on, if you're up for doing it, you can drive the bus. That's the big white van. We pick up at hospitals and bring the bodies back here. We pick up at private homes, as well, but for that we always send two representatives. If you're up for work in the Prep Room, dressing and so forth, I can give you more hours down the line. How does that sound?"

I had butterflies in my stomach, but I didn't let it show. I never had Brad's self-confidence, but I supposed I could fake it. "No problem."

Faking it is Lesson 36. The longer I spent in New York, the more I began to suspect that lots of people are faking it. They fake expertise at their jobs because no one wants to feel like a beginner. Everyone wants everyone else to know they know what they're doing. Everybody has an instant opinion on any subject even when they obviously don't know a damn thing about, say, how to fix the Middle East or how souvlaki is crushed into a hunk of meat that holds together on a spit.

Mostly, I think a lot of people are so fake all the time, they've forgotten what's up and what's real. And they're probably happier that way.

Ask a cabbie who drives the monied guys on Wall Street around and that taxi driver will tell you with certainty what stock to buy. Why not? His guess is as good as the guy studying quarterly projections and staring at stock tickers.

Lots of people fake it until they make it and by then they're successful experts making too much money. Too late to admit they're frauds then, isn't it? Illusions are everywhere and no one seems to notice. That's our everyday magic.

Lesson 37: However, #36 is only good practice for normal people. If you're a Normie, relax and do that. Be a fraud…unless you're a cardio-thoracic surgeon or something.

If you're one of us, however, any illusions you have about yourself can get you killed, or make you wish you were dead. People like us don't have the luxury of illusions when we're dealing with the Secret City. The Unseen has long, sharp teeth.

# 16

**M**y training for the role of door swinger included an expanded tour of the premises. Sam called the funeral home, "the sanctuary."

"The most important thing," Sam said, "is to know where the sanctuary's bathrooms are. Many of our guests are elderly and it is amazing how often they have to visit the facilities. Ladies, first on the right. Gentlemen, second on the right. Everything is wheelchair accessible, of course.

"I can't keep fancy, fragrant little soaps in the bathrooms," Sam complained. "I don't know if it's that they're wanting a keepsake from a loved one's funeral or if too many little old ladies are thieves. I have to stick to the liquid soap dispensers. And those are bolted to the wall."

The lilac wallpaper mimicked the lilac bouquet at the entrance to the Lilac Room. Each room was marked by a signature bouquet: the Rose Room, the Tulip Room and the Chrysanthemum Room.

Down the corridor from Sam's small office was a large conference room. She called it the Family Room. At its center was a rich mahogany table surrounded by deep leather chairs.

"This is the room where I make the arrangements with the families," Sam said. "It can take minutes or hours. It all depends on them. My rule is they get all the time they need to make the decisions they must make. Your mama is right, Tamara. Funerals are for the living. When you're out there doing pickups, you aren't just driving around those who have passed. We can't do anything more for them but show them respect. However, you are delivering compassion every time you meet a family. It's that important. This job isn't about shaking hands and driving corpses. This is a valuable opportunity to serve people when our service is most needed. Death is a vulnerable time and the families we serve need our help."

When I'd met Sam that morning, I wouldn't have suspected she had it in her to be so kind and compassionate. We all have our missions.

Next to the Family Room was the Display Room. An array of coffins sat ready. Some were beautiful and some were ugly. "Believe it or not," Sam said, "the cheapest caskets are the heaviest. Too much particle board. Try it."

I took the handle on one end and lifted it a few inches to gauge the casket's heft. I was glad of all the pushups Mr. Chang insisted upon and resolved to get back to doing them. I'd hiked all over New York and was confident in my cardio, but I'd taken too much time off from structured, weight-bearing exercise. I needed to get some kettlebells, too.

As if reading my mind, Sam asked if I worked out regularly. I told her I was getting back to it.

"Good," she said. "We serve three hundred families a

year here, but we handle the refrigeration and prep for another, larger funeral home, as well. Victor owns that one, too, so we actually handle closer to seven hundred bodies a year. There's hardly anyone here who doesn't have low back pain from all the lifting. I wish I could hire a massage therapist and a chiropractor to work in the back. We have the tables…but the tables are all stainless steel and have drains. Not very comfortable."

As cool as Sam could be when she was in manager mode, she was warm with people in grief. "Offer them water or tea or coffee," Sam said. "Water first, if they look agitated. I always suggest decaf at a funeral reception, but people rarely take good advice."

I worked my first funeral that same night. Sam was right. It was, oddly, very much like a party.

Brad's funeral had been more funereal and dour. On the other hand, Brad died a violent death at eighteen and Mrs. Ada Adams died at eighty-nine.

As I passed four women (who looked only slightly younger than Mrs. Adams) one of them whispered, "Pneumonia. She always had problems with her lungs. I told her she should see the doctor but she put me off. And now here she is."

"She looks nice, though," another hastened to put in.

"Oh, yeah," said the first. "She does look good. A vision in blue."

I hurried on. Over time I was to hear that conversation repeated with a hundred variations but with the same theme. Survivors whistle past the graveyard. "He shouldn't have eaten so much," or, "She must have felt a twinge of warning. She should have called an ambulance right away."

Lesson 38: The living blame the dead for dying. They look for reasons why the dead are gone because the survivors want to think they are safe. They're too sure they are such light sleepers, *they* would have awoken before the smoke strangled and the fire burned. The people left behind all want to believe they are exempt from entropy.

But those patterns emerged for me later. For that first funeral at Castille Funeral Services, the contrast between Mrs. Ada Adams' funeral and Brad's staggered me.

There were tears among a few of her contemporaries and Ada's grandchildren's eyes were wet. However, there was a lot of laughter, too.

A collage of photos showed Ada as a young woman. Here she was in black and white, graduating from high school. There was a faded photo of Ada at thirty-five or forty in a bright orange lifejacket. She's sitting in a rowboat toasting the camera with a bottle of beer. The last photo showed an array of birthday candles reflected in her huge glasses, moments before she was to make a wish and blow them out. She was eighty then. The woman she'd been, the one in the rowboat, had all but disappeared except for her bright blue eyes.

Lesson 39: Don't believe photos. They are posed and are meant to show us at our best. No life escapes pain, no matter what you see on the mantle over the fireplace or in the wedding album.

Photos at funerals can be especially deceptive. Collages of photos on easels are going out of style. It's usually a digital display of photos now, complete with music to make you feel worse. It seems like the soundtrack to all those snapshots of each lost life is always *Somewhere Over the Rainbow* and *What a Wonderful World*, by Israel

Kamakawiwo'ole. Cry along with the ukulele.

While we're at it, I'll hit you with Lesson 40 because I wasn't aware of it at the time and it turned out to be really important later. When we're young and somebody dies, we miss the departed, but Death is a scary mirror reflecting our fears. Lesson 40 is, if you can handle it or not, we're all running out of time. We hate funerals because it reminds us of what we've lost and what we will lose.

When Brad died, I confess, I thought less about him and more about us. I thought a lot about the future we'd lost together. I also felt really sorry for me.

I hate to admit it, but I blamed Brad a little bit, too. I wished he hadn't been messing around with farm machinery. I couldn't imagine how he'd lost both arms. It happens every year, always a shocking accident. I was mad at him for dying and leaving me and I don't like myself for that. Of course, I soon discovered he hadn't completely left, so there was more to be mad about, amid my wailing, moaning and crying.

Brad's casket had been closed. There was only one picture at his funeral and it was atop the casket. It was a picture of him as a little boy of eight wearing a green shirt and jeans, sitting on the farmhouse's front step. In the background, I could just spot the bottom of the door Brad would one day kick in as he made his way to the phone to call for help and for me.

Dents for dimples, of course, his funeral photo showed Brad smiling at the camera through crooked baby teeth. He was giving the camera a thumbs-up.

Looking at that photo, staring at his bright eyes, I saw the boy Brad had been, a long life ahead and nothing to worry about. I saw the son I might have had with Brad, too. I had hoped our children would inherit Brad's dimples. I didn't know at his funeral that I'd see my precious farm boy again soon enough, of course.

Ada Adams' casket was open. Her hands were folded neatly over her chest. Comparing the photos to the real thing, Ada's face looked a bit too long in death — "in repose," Sam called it.

"The dead don't bother me much," Samantha whispered to me, "but when I'm lying in bed at night and I cross my hands over my stomach like we cross the bodies' hands over their stomachs for display? I put my hands at my sides right away and try not to think about the big sleep. When I go, I want to be cremated, not posed and so forth."

I began by greeting people at the door and directing them back to the Lilac Room where the body waited to be viewed and reviewed.

The trick to greeting people at a visitation is not to say, "How are you?" It's reflexive. We ask strangers how they are every day, not wanting to know. Ask a widow that and you'll get what you deserve when she replies, "Considering I just lost my husband of forty years, how do you think I am, moron?"

At a visitation, the door swinger's main job is to refrain from saying, "How are you?" and direct visitors to the appropriate room. There were four rooms, but for Ada's funeral, the smallest, the Lilac Room, was of sufficient size.

It seemed the whole town of Medicament came out for Brad's funeral. For Ada, we hosted a little over thirty guests. It seemed a small, grim turnout for such a long life, but perhaps she'd already outlived many friends who

106

would have come to pay their respects.

I unfolded chairs and helped to set them up in rows. Sam showed me how the coffee machine worked.

The service was officiated by the son of the deceased. I'd assumed all these ceremonies were presided over by a priest or a minister, but Sam informed me that Mrs. Adams had been a freethinker and did not ascribe to any religion. The final visitation was to be brief, followed by a short memorial service.

Still, the service was sweet and one of the granddaughters sang a song of her own composition. The service was kind of like church, but I liked it more because I didn't have to sit still for very long.

One lonely looking guest in particular got my attention. He was shaven carelessly. No one spoke to him and he spoke to no one. He stood at the head of the casket and gazed down into Ada's face.

"Can I get you some water or tea, sir?" Of course, too late I realized I was speaking to a ghost in front of everyone.

Lesson 41: Give everyone a good look before you strike up a conversation. Look for pale complexions, open sores, wounds, recently stitched wounds, transparency, and mournful stares.

None of the above was present with the guy standing at Ada's casket so I might have missed the signs anyway. You've probably already spoken with a ghost and didn't know it. The guy who ignores you at a party? Yeah, assume all those guys are ghosts. Sometimes, especially with the ghosts of the cremated, it's hard to tell.

I've since been informed that the idea that cremation leaves a ghost's appearance clean and less wormy and decayed is the way it worked in the movie, *The Frighteners,* starring Michael J. Fox. Go watch that for further tips on how things are. It's not terribly far off from the way it really is.

Or watch any Michael J. Fox movie. The thought of Michael J. Fox in a fun movie might, for instance, be a happy distraction next time you make the mistake of lying in bed, staring at the ceiling and crossing your hands over your stomach. Unless we become ghosts, we'll all be in that position, in repose, for eternity.

Ghost, burnt or lying very still forever…not much of a choice is it?

# 17

**T**he ghost's hand snaked out fast and touched my hand. An electrical shock went up my arm and I felt dizzy. As I reached out with my free hand to steady myself, my palm brushed Ada Adams's shoulder.

I saw a flash of white light and I wasn't standing in the funeral home anymore. I stood in a circle of flowers. As the light dimmed slightly, I saw that I was in a garden surrounded by white orchids. They were all one kind and they trembled in the warm breeze.

I blinked and the man stood before me again. He was younger now. He had all his hair, which was parted in the middle. I giggled at him.

"Who gave you that haircut, Todd?" I asked. "You should get your money back."

"Ada?"

To my surprise, I said, "Yes?"

"I want to thank you. You kept my secret all those years, even after I died."

I felt a wave of regret sweep over me. "I shouldn't have, but blood is blood. You swore to me you wouldn't do it again and you did. You reap what you sow, Todd."

"I understand that now, Ada. You have your rest, but I don't. I'll never be able to rest until you tell the Other."

"Now? Why now?" I asked.

"I want to rest."

"It's all too little, too late."

"No! Ada! *Please!*"

"You really think you'll be set free?"

"Even if I'm not, it's the right thing. And there is Carl. He's still doing it. What was in me has got him now. Those girls…tell the Other, for their sake. Maybe even for Carl's sake. You know it's the right thing. I love you, Ada."

"Oh, Todd. You were the worst brother a girl could ever have."

For a moment, I was Ada. I was me, as well. When Todd, the poorly shaven ghost spoke to his sister, they spoke of The Other. In a flash, I understood that The Other was none other than me, Tamara Smythe, newbie ghost channeler.

I was confused. I was at Castille Funeral Home but I also stood briefly in a circle of white orchids talking to my murdering brother.

There was much more to Ada's life than the collage of photos by her casket suggested. She was a murderer, too, but she had attained rest while her brother Todd had not.

Then Todd was gone and I stood beside Ada. She turned to me, touched my cheek and said gently, "I'm sorry."

Then she confessed everything, for her brother and a nephew named Carl.

I sorted all this out later, but first, a word about channeling murderous ghosts:

Lesson 42: When sent reeling out of a powerful vision, try not to throw up in an open casket. Aim for your shoes.

# 18

**M**y eyes fluttered open. I was on the couch in Sam's office with a cold, wet towel on the back of my head. My skull throbbed with pain.

Sam's voice drifted down to me with all the softness of a rain of thumbtacks and baseballs. "Tamara? Can you hear me?"

"Urgh," I said.

"She lost consciousness, Doctor," Sam said. "I think we should get her to the hospital."

"I'm okay," I said. My throat was dry. "How long was I out?"

"Just long enough for us to get you to the office and for someone to fetch my bag from my car," a man said. He was taking my pulse and I glimpsed the little black bag at his feet. A stethoscope was draped around his neck.

The doctor felt the back of my head with probing fingers, palpating in a way that wasn't so gentle that it could do no good.

"Do you know your name?" he asked.

"Tamara Smythe."

"Do you know where you are?"

"At Castille, in Sam's office, feeling horribly embarrassed."

The doctor laughed. "It happens. I knew a med student once who couldn't stand the sight of earwax. Blood? He was fine with blood. But digging earwax potatoes out of someone's blocked ear canal? He couldn't handle it. Put him off his food and he lost far too much weight in short order. He made it through med school with flying colors and never went near anyone's ear canal again. And do you know what that guy does now? He's the top proctologist in Michigan."

"It was your first funeral," Sam said.

"Second."

"It was your first here."

"Was it my last here?" I asked.

"Yes," Sam said. "This was your last night."

"I'm so sorry. In front of all those people...I...oh, god." I could still taste the vomit. I blushed and covered my face with my hands. "I've never lost a job before. And I'll never eat shawarma again. Oh...."

"It's all fine, Tamara," Sam said. "I'm just glad we had a doctor in the house. This is Dr. Brooks."

The man smiled. "Pleased to meet you, Tamara. Any history of fainting spells?"

"No."

"How's your head feel?"

"The pain is already going away." It wasn't, but I wanted them to back off and give me some breathing room and time to think.

"Well, I could send you in for some tests or you could leave it a little and see how you feel. Any more dizziness?"

113

"No."

"Are you on any drugs?"

"No."

"What did you eat today?"

"Not much. It's my first day on the job and I just had a little shawarma, which…like I said…"

"Yeah, yeah. Maybe we should get you a sports drink. Make sure your electrolyte levels are happy, hm? Have you been under a lot of stress?"

"Yeah. I guess."

"Can you shrug your shoulders for me, Tamara?"

I did.

"How about a smile? A forced one will do as long as it's even on both sides of your face."

I complied and the doctor nodded. "And raise both arms above your head…yes, no problem there. Any ringing in your ears?"

"No."

"How's your blood pressure?"

"It's a little low. Sometimes if I get up too quickly I see spots."

"Well, there you go. Probably just the emotion of the moment and proximity to the body. It happens, usually on the first day of cadaver lab in any med school. Some kids discover syncope their first day of high school biology when they have to dissect a worm or a frog. Tamara, what you've experienced is something that's quite common among young people close to your age. You'd be surprised."

"What have I got?" (I meant, of course, what have I got besides the ability to see ghosts and drain them of information about their sins?)

"You've just had an episode of vasovagal syncope. Something triggers you and *bam!* You fall down. That's the main concern with fainting, the falling down part," the doctor assured me. "Once you're safely on the floor, blood flow returns to the brain and the confusion lifts and here you are."

"This sucks!" I said.

"Oh, it could be much worse, believe me. Maybe now you know what careers aren't for you, hm? Funeral parlors aren't your thing, I think."

I felt miserable and was on the brink of tears. "I was thinking about being a doctor someday. Instead, I'm...I don't know what I'm doing!"

He shrugged. "Maybe there's something else out there that would suit you better. Do you want to sit up and see how that works for you? Slowly, now."

"Yes. Thank you. I can't imagine what everyone thought."

Sam rolled her eyes. "I can."

Dr. Brooks laughed easily again. "No, no. It's really fine. The family was just concerned for you, that's all. Everyone was worried."

"Yeah, everybody but Carl," I said.

"What do you mean?" the doctor asked.

"I had a...thought. It's nothing. He...."

As soon as I was up, my breathing got shorter and I felt fuzzy over my heart and head. I recognized this feeling. I'd had it when the Sheriff told me Brad was dead. I was about to have a panic attack. Extended contact with ghosts and getting messages from beyond Death is not for sissies.

The doctor smiled. "What were you going to say,

Tamara?"

"She's had a quite knock, Doctor. I'll get someone to drive her home."

"Sometimes what comes up from the unconscious can be significant." Dr. Brooks pressed. "What did you think happened when you were unconscious?"

"I had a vision, for lack of a better word."

"Oh, *gawd*," Sam said.

And everything I knew spilled out. "I spoke to a man who was standing by the casket. I offered him a drink. He was an older man with a lousy shave who hurt young girls. He killed one of them. I found out…I mean…Ada…his sister. *She* found out. In Queens. He made her promise to keep his secret or he'd kill her, too."

Sam put her hands over her eyes and moaned. "Oh, Victor, what have you saddled me with?"

"Ada said she wouldn't tell, but he had to stop."

Dr. Brooks stared at me. His expression did not change. "Tamara? Do you have a history of mental illness? Have you ever been hospitalized for a mental disorder?"

I stood up. "It's true. You don't have to believe me, but I know it's true. There are two bodies, behind a wall in an old house in Queens. The second body will be in a battered old freezer in the basement. There are cartons of ice cream over top of the body of the girl. When police find them, they'll be wrapped in plastic and all their teeth will be missing. There are more bodies under the floor."

"Oh," Dr. Brooks said.

"Yes. And that's not all. When the old lady discovered her brother's secret, she sewed him up in his bedsheets while he was asleep after going to bed drunk and injected him with too much insulin. Todd hardly had his diabetes

116

under control, anyway. She made it look like a suicide. The cops found him in bed after she tidied up the scene. She murdered him rather than admit to the cops that she could have stopped her brother before he killed again."

"I should call someone," Sam said. She opened a filing cabinet drawer. "I've got Victor's number here somewhere."

I whirled on Sam. "It gets worse. Todd was a serial killer, but his son has the same sick tastes. Todd and Ada are dead and gone, but Carl is still out there. When the cops dig under that house in Queens, they're going to find Carl's victims, too."

The doctor put his stethoscope in his bag and stood. "Okay. That's enough. I'll take her in my car over to Bellevue. Don't worry, Mrs. Biggs. You'll never be bothered by this young woman again. I'll sign her in myself and I'll talk to the family. After a steep discount on your services, I can *probably* talk the family out of the worst Yelp review in the history of Yelp reviews of funeral homes."

"No," Sam said, still digging through the filing cabinet. "Tamara is my responsibility. My boss won't be happy if I let her out of my sight."

That's when I felt the cold blade of the scalpel at my throat. A scalpel is a small thing, but it's designed for cruel cutting. I felt the doctor's hot breath at my ear.

"After my father's suicide, I changed my name. *I'm* Carl. You don't seem to understand what I'm capable of. In a moment, I'm tempted to show you."

Sam's head came up and her eyes widened. "What you don't seem to understand, Doctor, is I found the file I was looking for. *G* is for gun." She pulled a small silver pistol

117

into view and pointed it at his head.

He ducked down behind me and held me tight. "I'll slit her throat." I felt the blade's bite as warm blood trickled from the beginning of the incision under my left ear. I was sure he would make one sure, sweeping cut that would end under my right ear. "Drop that gun. I swear I'll kill her."

"Then she'll fall to the floor and I'll have a clear shot, won't I?"

"I'll cut her head off!"

"Shoot him," I said.

Dr. Brooks shoved me toward Sam and ran from the room. I collapsed back to the couch rather than knock her over.

However, Sam did not shoot. She shook as she crossed the room. She looked down the hall to make sure he was gone.

We both heard the pounding of running feet and the pleasant chime at the front entrance. The door slammed behind him. Sam turned the lock on her office door. Her knees were still shaking as she sat in a chair. She looked so pale, I thought she might faint, too.

"'*G* is for gun?' Really?" I managed a smile before I started crying.

Sam pulled the magazine from the pistol grip, shook it and shrugged. The weapon was not loaded. "Good thing he didn't know bullets are filed under *B*." Sam cried, too.

Then, through our tears, we began to laugh together. That's how I made my second friend in New York.

Lesson 43: You never really know what's going on until after it happens.

# 19

After a quick trip to the bathroom, a gargle and a splash of water in my face, I was in the passenger seat of a hearse.

Sam drove but couldn't seem to stop herself from lecturing. "For future reference, you made a rookie mistake. When someone is at the casket paying their respects, they are in the bubble of quiet reflection. Don't offer them comfort, coffee or tea until they move at least ten feet from the casket and their backs are turned to the body."

"Does this mean I still have a job?"

"Technically, Tammy, I think you have two jobs. I'm taking you to the second one now. Do you know the address where the bodies of those girls are?"

"No. It's like a dream. The technical details are already receding."

"Understandable. I'm good at math," she said, "but have you ever tried to do math in your dreams?"

"No," I said. "That's weird."

"Well, I've tried it and it's impossible."

"I can picture the house. If I saw it again, I'd know it."

"Good. You may be called upon to do so."

She turned a corner and wove through thick traffic easily. "This is what I love about driving the coach," she said. "People give way and give the meat wagon respect. Even in this city."

I glanced behind me into the rear of the hearse. "We're riding empty."

"Yeah, but they don't know there's no body in back. People are superstitious."

"From what I've seen," I said, "they ought to be. How long have you been seeing ghosts?"

Sam spared me a glance. "Oh, I don't. I leave that to... people like you. Victor's people. I leave that stuff to you *gladly*."

"Yeah. I haven't gotten to the point where it's a fun party trick yet."

"Victor says a war is coming. When the secret is out, he says, 'There will be Hell to pay.' I think he means that expression literally."

I didn't know what to make of that so I put the warning aside. "It just occurred to me that this is the second time this year a man has tried to kill me. They were both doctors. How am I ever going to get a checkup again?"

"Yeah, I'd be too paranoid to get in the stirrups if I were you."

"Sam!"

"Sorry. Joke."

"Well, yeah, but how will I?"

"I'll give you the name of my gyno. She delivered my kids and I haven't seen her sacrifice a goat in her waiting room yet. How did the first one try to kill you?"

"Strangulation. To be fair, I was threatening to rip open his throat with a pen at the time. Long story. That sounds worse than it was. I mean, it sounds awful but, believe it or not, I was the good guy in that situation."

The tires squealed and the engine growled as Sam wheeled around a tight corner. "All of Victor's people are good as far as I can tell. I'll take your word for it."

"You keep saying Victor's people. What do you mean by that? I thought you were one of Victor's people."

"I'm the chocolate icing on the cake that hides the fact that it's really a mud pie. I'm part of the funding side of things, but I don't work the underside of the city. If I were expecting the dark side to show up at Castille, I'd have kept my gun loaded. I always thought this stuff was for Victor's people to deal with. I'm a regular citizen," Sam said. "My job is to keep pretending everything's okay."

"Everything's not okay?"

"Do you read the news?"

"Nope."

She sighed. "Youth."

"Sam, are we going to try to find Carl Brooks in Queens?"

She stepped on the brakes. Tall warehouses surrounded us and I guessed we were in the Meatpacking District. These dark hulks didn't seem to house lofts or businesses. They were just anonymous, boarded up buildings that looked like they might be condemned at any moment.

Sam picked up her phone and dialed a number. A steel gate across the street slid back to reveal a narrow alley. As soon as the opening was wide enough, Sam shot the car through the gap.

"I'm still a civilian and aim to stay that way," Sam said.

"But you'll need backup. My understanding is there's usually a training and orientation period. Sounds to me like you're already swimming at the deep end of the pool."

Sam turned left at the end of the alley and the lane widened. Ahead, at the bottom of one of the warehouses, I saw a line of light growing as we approached. The entrance to a parking garage yawned open.

"Sam? Why do you keep the secret? That ghosts are real, I mean?" I was distraught. I thought the trouble was just ghosts. I'd forgotten Lesson 13. Remember Lesson 13? Civilization lives and breathes as it is because of the power of denial. As strong as denial is, I didn't understand then how brittle denial can be. Trees stand a long time because they bend to the wind. Just like old trees, rigidity leads to the fall of civilizations.

Sam parked the hearse and turned off the engine. "Why do I keep the secret? Because it's crazy. Because ghosts aren't the half of it. Because, *ha!* You think people argue about religion *now*? There'd be religious wars. A lot of religion is relatively harmless now, and even does a lot of good, partly because people don't take it too seriously. If people start to understand the forces that are here, among us, trying to burst through? Wow. We'd have a lot more fundamentalists running around spouting the one true way and killing anyone who disagrees."

"You're that sure people can't handle the truth?" As soon as I said it, I thought Sam might break out her Jack Nicholson impression for the obligatory *A Few Good Men* reference.

She didn't take the bait. Sam looked me in the eye, deadly serious. "I'm sure. Most of them can't handle a snowstorm. Wait till you see what happens if the word really gets out and boneheads start to worry about the nature of existence. These deep questions are what sports, politics, the stock market, television, Twitter, Facebook and arguing about movies over lattes is *for*, kid! The nonsense is here to distract us from thinking about what's waiting at the end of our short little earthly ride.

"The system works because we hardly think about what's next. We bury our concerns, six feet down, and pretend. I never want to *stop* pretending. No one does."

# 20

Sam gave the hearse's horn two, long blasts and the sound bounced around the unlit parking garage. It felt like we were alone in a cave.

"You know, lots of people already suspect the truth. I'm not alone in keeping the secret." Sam said. "Victor says the Underworld is rising up and spilling into our world. That's one reason why there are more suicide bombers in the world lately."

"What's the other reason?"

"There are many. Mainly poverty. Poverty is a weapon of mass destruction."

"Um. Okay."

"My point is, we're building *toward* something. What Victor calls the Evil Quotient is rising again."

"The Evil Quotient?"

"Of course. It rises and falls, but it's a thing, like how there were very few serial killers in the United States and over a few decades their numbers built up until we were hip deep in them."

"Um...what do you mean by that quotient rising

*again?*"

"According to Victor's people, it's cyclical. They say everything is."

"So when was the Evil Quotient high before?"

"They argue about that. Star positions and high math are involved. Maybe it was the Dark Ages or maybe the George Bush administration."

"That's a lot of latitude."

"Yeah. Not an exact science. Witches argue like bitches, apparently. They argue about carrying the two or something. Anyway, Victor says more people have seen ghosts or had an intuition of them as things get worse, *measurably*. The theory is that it's because the Underworld and the Overworld are getting closer to each other. Like they say in *Ghostbusters*, 'Don't cross the streams!'"

"I really should see that movie."

"You're kidding, right?"

I shook my head.

"And here I thought you were something special. Maybe you aren't ready for Adult Swim, after all." She let out a girlish giggle. Or maybe she was on the edge of hysteria, I couldn't say for sure.

"If you're on the outside, how do you know all this?"

She sighed. "Victor and I used to be lovers. No secrets in bed. And he needs people like me to help keep his empire funded. I don't know for sure, but maybe a quarter of the managers of his businesses know the truth."

"What is the truth?"

"The truth is that reality is even scarier than we thought. We can't handle that."

"Maybe we could if given the chance."

Sam looked at me for a moment. I thought she was

considering my idea. I was wrong. She was formulating an argument why no one must ever know about ghosts.

"Did you know that nearly eight in ten Americans believe in angels?" Sam asked. "That's a real statistic."

My eyes widened. "Are you saying angels are real?"

Sam snorted. "Oh, Iowa. Let the scales fall from your eyes. People believe in angels because they want to think there is hope. They're desperate for hope and lottery wins. When people get glimpses of the Underworld, they think they see an angel because people need comfort. They want their world to make sense in a *benevolent* way. That's why climate change deniers get so much traction. They're soothing to the nerves."

"Oh, I don't know — "

Sam shook her head harder. "People don't want to see a scary world unless it's Sunday night when *The Walking Dead* comes on. When ordinary people see ghosts, that's the gap between Under and Over closing. They glimpse a scary thing and they want to *think* that apparition is an angel. There's no comfort in knowing it's your crazy Aunt Sadie who died in a fertilizer factory explosion and is now doomed to walk the Earth for some reason no one understands. People love certainty. They prefer it to truth nine times out of ten. If the ethereal meets the concrete and the secret really gets out, the looting and the self-righteous condemnation might not ever stop."

"What do you think would happen?"

"We talk a good game about Good and Evil. If everyone knew and acknowledged in their hearts that our dead relatives are still here and watching us? The freak out would go on and on. Society is fragile, Tamara. All the churches and sects and cults would go to war over which one true religion will keep us from becoming ghosts. Well…nobody can get a burger and a decent cup of coffee in the ideologue apocalypse."

Lesson 44: Our way of life, and coffee, are threatened. The stakes are very high.

I worked it through in my head. I thought of Brad's father piling more mashed potatoes on his plate last Christmas and worrying aloud that India and Pakistan have nuclear weapons. I pictured Mama leading a platoon of Presbyterians in a firefight with the local Seventh Day Adventists. "Jesus!" I said finally.

"I'm unclear on how He may be involved," she deadpanned.

"Did you practice that speech?" I asked.

"No. I just talked about it many times with Victor. He wanted to recruit me to the cause. He and his mystics tried to train me in the 'Art of Seeing the Unseen.' Turns out I don't have the knack. And given what I do for a living, I'm grateful. I don't want that superpower, thanks. You do you, Boo." Sam took a deep breath but it was still shaky as she let it out. "Any questions?"

"You and Victor, huh?"

Sam laughed. She laughed a lot. It was that edgy, nervous laugh I'd heard from some residents at Shibboleth that conveyed: *I'm not crazy. I'm just on the edge of crazy and everything's fine, everything's fine, everything's okay…crazy? Who? Me?* She laughed the way people laugh on roller coasters, shaking and nervous and maybe on the edge of losing bladder control.

"Don't wrinkle your nose over me and Victor," Sam said. "He's an elegant man and I love the way he speaks. When we had sex, he only spoke Spanish. It was wow."

"Wow."

"And pow. It was a long time ago, before I had kids… and only slightly after I met the man who became my husband."

"Oh."

"Yeah. Oh."

"What happens now?"

"I don't know and I won't know. I'm dropping you off. Regular citizen, remember? I'm a civilian. Keep your military secrets to yourself."

"But — "

"Tamara. Look at me. When I was a kid a little younger than you, I was going to be a marine biologist. I like whales. Then my father died and I went to his funeral and he didn't look like himself. He looked like a wax doll. The cosmetologist did a terrible job. My father didn't look like my father. He looked like a poor imitation of my father under a yellow light.

"That picture of my dad — that last picture — is the only thing that haunts me. So while my best friends from high school went off to become lawyers and dentists and chiropractors, I ended up studying Mortuary Science. My last memory of my dad before we buried him is all the haunting I want in my life."

I nodded. "But, if you're a civilian, what does that make me?"

Sam and I both jumped, nerves jangling, as my door opened. I looked up into a face I recognized. It was Victor's driver, the huge man with the cauliflower ears and the bent nose. He stood holding the door open with one hand. His other hand held a collapsed black and red umbrella. "You're late," he said.

"I didn't even know I had an appointment," I said.

He smiled, revealing that two upper front teeth were gold plated. His eyes were a gray that made me think of wolves. His sort of face was a guarantee that, under that expensive suit he was packed into, his body was a road map of muscles and veins and aggressive tattoos.

"Mr. Fuentes has finished his conference with the coven. He is waiting for you in the library, Ms. Smythe. Welcome to the Choir Invisible."

Lesson 45: People will say some ridiculous stuff to you. Keep a straight face in case the impossible turns out to be real. If you don't react to news, people will think you're smarter and cooler than you really are. That's okay as long as you don't fool yourself, too.

# 21

**S**am gave me one quick wave. "If you survive the night, I'll have more work for you. Call me." She revved the hearse's engine and pulled out of the parking garage in a hurry.

"Wow. That was kind of cold," I said.

The big man spoke with a clipped accent that I guessed might be Russian. "Samantha is afraid. She knows the truth but prefers the lie. She stands with many."

"I got that."

"Her first child is Victor's son, but Samantha and her husband Bryce prefer to pretend that Victor is not the father."

"Dude! Do you say everything that comes to mind?"

"Jesus said the truth shall set us free."

"They crucified him."

"You have a point. Samantha does not like me. I think she is pretty. She does not think I am pretty."

"There's something really dysfunctional about you. I'm not sure what it is yet. Are you a robot?"

He looked down at himself and appeared to consider

the question seriously. "To my knowledge, no. However, if I were a robot who was programmed without self-knowledge, and if, perhaps, I was a cyborg with organic components that could bleed and feel pain...it is possible I am a robot. I don't think it likely, but it is possible we are all robots." He pronounced the word *possible* as if he was saying *pissable*.

"You're starting to freak me out. Who are you?"

"Apologies. I am Vladimir Estasia. Please call me Vlad."

When he said *please*, he pronounced it *pliss*. My hand disappeared into his calloused palm as we shook hands and I felt an electrical shock pass between us. The feeling lingered longer than a quick spark of static electricity and I felt an uncomfortable tingling race up my arm.

Vlad held on a little too long and only let go when I ripped my hand from his grasp.

"You have suffered a terrible loss," he said. "I am sorry." A single tear tracked down his cheek. "*Terrible.*"

"Yes...uh, thanks. How did you know that?"

Vlad shrugged and wiped the tear away with scarred knuckles. "It is written on your nerves. I am sorry. I should have asked first before slipping into a reading. It is not often that I encounter such a deep love. You loved your young man so very much."

"I did."

"It is a tragic love."

"It was good while it lasted."

"That's not what I meant," Vlad said. "I mean you loved and continue to love him but all he has now is rage and resentment. He will not be free until you set him free."

131

"*What?*"

Vlad bent his head and closed his eyes. "Not what. Who. You."

"What?"

"No. *Who*. Or whom. Pardon my English. You must ask your young man's forgiveness. His circumstance in the place between worlds is partially your fault."

I looked him up and down and spoke through clenched teeth. "You should take your act over to Coney Island, man. There's another lousy medium on the Boardwalk you could trade fortunes with and skin the rubes."

He shrugged. "I am rarely wrong. Your nerves — "

"You've got your wires crossed this time. And I'm starting to think I should kick your ass."

"That would be unlikely." He cocked his head. "Though you do have that potential in you, Tamara. Big does not matter. Small does not matter. Conviction is all that matters. You know this, I think. Mr. Chang trained you well."

My jaw dropped. I took a deep breath and let it out slowly. "Let's go see Victor, shall we? Before we find out what I might be capable of."

Lesson 46: Check your blind spot.

## 22

Our footsteps echoed as I followed Vlad through the parking garage. It was by far the quietest place I'd been in New York City. The garage looked unremarkable at first and too dark to make out much more than the shapes of cars. I caught rich odors of grease and fuel.

Closer to the elevator, where the light was better, I could see the garage contained a collection of vehicles. Large trucks and a couple of Land Rovers shone under spotlights. Several nondescript automobiles lined a far wall. Occupying a place of honor under bright gallery lights, a couple of shiny motorcycles sat together with helmets hanging from their handlebars. Beyond them, in the darkness, I could just make out the silhouette of a good sized boat. "If I remember correctly, you're missing a dinosaur replica and a huge penny."

"I beg your pardon?" Vlad said.

"This is the Batcave, right?"

"It is not."

I shrugged. "My boyfriend was into comics. I'm guessing you aren't."

"I am not."

I recognized Victor's white limo. It sat between two more limousines, one black and the other silver. Everything was shiny.

Far off to my left, I saw the car collection's crowning glory. It was one of those sports cars that are slung so low, they look like potholes could destroy them. It shone under spotlights. Brad would have loved those cars. He loved machinery of all sorts. (Then it occurred to me that, in the end, machinery had not loved him back.)

Vlad pushed the button for the elevator, a narrow cylinder made of ornate brass. I asked him if his boss planned on having a yard sale soon.

Vlad studied my face for a moment and said, "I suspect you are a *leetle* funny."

"Just a *leetle*," I replied.

Vlad and I squeezed into the little elevator and I could smell his aftershave. It was too heavy and reminded me of the few cabs I'd been in.

I pressed against the wall of the elevator car. I wanted to make sure I didn't accidentally touch Vlad's hand and get another impromptu bullshit reading.

As the elevator rattled and shimmied up one floor, I thought of Brad shaving. When he was fresh from the shower, his cheeks were smooth as a baby's. I loved to hug him tight and kiss his chin and smell that faint scent.

Brad bought his shaving cream in a cheap can from the Dollar Holler. Lime. When I thought of Brad, I could almost smell the lime. I made a mental note to buy myself a cheap can of shaving cream, just for the soft and safe memories.

Then I looked up into Vlad's eyes and made up Lesson

47.

Lesson 47: when you're in the presence of someone who might be a real mind reader, try to do math equations. Dividing by seven is good. Fractions are helpful. Failing that, you might try thinking of dead kittens. Try to think of anything else so you don't think about sex.

Which you will. Bad news: No matter how much math you do, when you stand next to a clairvoyant and you know it, your mind goes to what you don't want them to know. Prepare to be embarrassed and hope they can be discreet.

From the outside, the building had looked like an anonymous hulk. The floor above the garage was not just a dark warehouse. The second floor reminded me of the lobby of the Waldorf Astoria Hotel.

I had never stayed at the Waldorf, of course, but in my first days of exploring New York, I had walked into the lobby. I'd hoped to see the train car on the track beneath the hotel. Presidents had taken the secret trolley to the hotel for privacy and security. A tourist website reported that it was rumored the artist, Andy Warhol, had fabulous, drug-fueled parties down there.

It seemed too weird and specific a detail to be coy about. Did Warhol have parties on the secret train car beneath the Waldorf Astoria or not?

I never found out for sure. The lobby looked too luxurious and the patrons had the air of wealth and privilege. The place was too rich for me to breathe the air. I walked in, saw the huge chandelier and turned around immediately, feeling too out of place and undeserving to stand around gawking at fancy marble columns.

I'd wanted to feel like a real New Yorker but, at the

Waldorf, I felt like I was naked except for being draped in Iowa's state flag. I thought the concierge might check to make sure I was wearing shoes. I didn't belong at the Waldorf Astoria and I was sure everyone knew it. As I followed Vlad through the warehouse's second floor, I felt like I was back in the lobby of the Waldorf.

I mentioned that, to appear cool, you should look bored. Don't let your jaw go slack or allow your eyes to widen. Look like nothing can surprise or impress you. I didn't manage it that night, but maybe you could.

The place was divided into vast, dark rooms. (The word *room* seemed too small a word for what I witnessed.) I passed a music room that seemed to house two of every musical instrument. A Noah's Ark for brass, percussion and woodwinds, it was as if they stood ready to fornicate to repopulate the Earth if all other instruments were carried away in a flood.

Several rooms were stacked and packed from the floor to the high ceilings with cardboard boxes. I glimpsed markings on the sides of the cartons that read: MREs.

Farther down the corridor was a gymnasium. A room to the left was filled with weights, treadmills and gymnastic equipment. The training mat took up the dimensions of a tennis court, four times the size of Mr. Chang's dojang back in Medicament.

To the right stood another room dedicated to swords. Vlad paused and turned on a light. Three spotlights high in the ceiling lit the polished hardwood floor in broad, glowing circles. One wall was decorated with swords of many shapes and sizes. There were spears and knives, too. "The Blade Room," Vlad said. "Perhaps the most important room for you."

"I've never touched a real sword with an edge," I said. "Just kendo and wooden practice swords."

"My favorite is the pata." Vlad propped his umbrella by the door and walked to a rack. He pulled out a short sword. It did not have a hilt. Vlad put his hand *into* the handle and a metal sheath protected his hand and wrist.

"The *pata* is a gauntlet sword," Vlad explained. "It is an Indian invention, traditionally used in pairs, one for each hand."

The light from the Blade Room leaked across the corridor. Dueling pistols hung crossed at the barrels on the wall at the gun room's entrance. That was quaint. Then I spotted the display of rifles and automatic weapons. This was not a museum collection. *Decorated, array and display* weren't the right words. This was a fortress and *that* was an arsenal.

"This building is a storehouse for many supplies," Vlad said. "The complex is four buildings in all. Together, we call these warehouses the Keep. They form a square and take up the block."

"How long has it taken Victor to put this together?"

"Several lives and his lifetime."

"What do you mean, 'several lives?' Do you mean, like, past lives?"

"Heh. No."

I felt the strong suspicion that Vlad might be incapable of lying. However, in his obsession for truth telling, condescension crept into his voice, too. He seemed immune to my dirty looks, blissfully unaware of his ability to offend.

As we climbed a spiral staircase, he continued, "Things cost money. Some things cost more than money. On the top floor, there are objects that hold power from a long time ago. It costs lives to dig things up that are buried very deep down. When these items see sunlight and moonlight again, there are people who would kill to get those things."

"Thanks for the tour," I said, "but I'm in a hurry to talk to Victor. There's a doctor in Queens who's going to get away if we don't do something about it. He has done terrible things."

Vlad shook his huge head. "Terrible. It is much easier to find the energy of evil after it has taken life than to divine its purpose before it strikes. Evil is always striking, a hammer to an anvil, but we know not where the blows will next fall."

"Let's just call the cops. An anonymous tip."

"Victor will have other ideas."

"Why?"

"Because he is the smartest of us."

The hallways on the third floor were narrow and all the doors were closed. The light was just as dim and the air was cold. A space as vast as the Keep seemed impossible to heat.

Vlad seemed to know his way through the maze, but I couldn't understand how. I just followed his broad back and hoped he could find his way while I pulled out my phone.

Soon, the hallway ahead brightened. When I looked up from my cell, we were on a narrow metal catwalk high above another large space. We had crossed the boundary from one warehouse into a connecting warehouse.

As dark as the first warehouse had been, this space was very bright and warm. The floor below us was part farm, part jungle. Several workers wearing what looked like

Hazmat suits worked in a glass greenhouse. All the light was artificial and I had to shield my eyes.

"What is this place? Are you growing plants for drugs or something?"

"Some of the plants are medicinal. Most are for food. This is the Greenhouse."

"Why?"

"Contingency plans. Enough to feed a small army. I can tell the truth about the past and the present. Sadly, the future is not my specialty. We hope we won't need all these..." — he waved his hand in a vague way that suggested to me he had no interest in the project below.

"No roses down there," he said. "No room! I wish there was room for roses. If the end comes, I want roses. I want light pink roses."

I looked at him skeptically. "Pink? For a big bruiser like you?"

"Pink roses represent admiration, gentleness, sweetness and joy."

"Is that you?"

"I would like it to be me," he said. "Many of the others in the Choir, all they can think of is Death. They would surround themselves with bouquets of black roses. The black rose is the death rose. Death is our business, but we are still alive. We should remember and enjoy."

Knowing he would tell the truth, I asked Vlad what rose he would recommend for me.

He answered without hesitation. "For you? I would give a dark red rose. Dark red roses convey unconscious beauty. There is time enough for black roses later."

I don't think Vlad meant to creep me out, but that, "unconscious beauty" thing made me self-conscious. The "black roses later," remark sounded pretty ominous, too.

When we left the catwalk I gave one last glance behind me. The Keep's contents suggested the Choir Invisible — whatever they were up to — expected a war. The workings of the Greenhouse somehow scared me more. Growing food in secret in the middle of New York City was too Bond villain for me.

Sam spoke of the apocalypse and the concept obviously terrified her. I wondered if Victor, with his vast stores, would welcome the end of the world as we know it (whatever form the end might take). If the end came, Victor could be a king.

Lesson 48: Lots of people dream of the apocalypse. They ache for it but they don't understand the totality of their fondest wish. They imagine remaking the world according to their own rules (except everyone wants their own rules.) They imagine the sweet pleasures of shooting guns all day at zombies that don't shoot back. Or maybe they predict they will shoot up to heaven while they mock the boss they hate for being trapped among the damned.

Everybody loves escapism, but when Armageddon really hits, no one escapes. Especially not people like you and me.

# 23

The third building on the tour was a vast windowless library. Tall wooden shelves bowed under the weight of thick, old books.

"You like?" Vlad asked.

"Haven't you people ever heard of a kindle or an iPad? It would save a lot of trees."

"These books are not for sale anywhere. They are the fables and legends and myths and forgotten religious texts of history. We are working on putting them all online for faster reference. Victor believes the secrets to winning the war might be hidden here somewhere, perhaps in a leather scroll of ancient spells, crumbling and cracking." Vlad shrugged. "Most of it is probably a bunch of bullshit."

"*Boolsheet*," I echoed Vlad. "Dude, I love the way you express yourself."

He glanced my way. "I might be offended, thinking you are mocking me. However, I can see when you are telling the truth. I amuse you. I am pleased."

"Yes. You're Louis C.K. and Chris Rock put together."

"Now you are being disingenuous, but in a lighthearted manner. I am not offended. I prefer Jon Stewart. He has an appreciation for the absurd and he is always trying to tell the truth as he sees it."

As we came to the center of the library, the longest table I'd ever seen stretched back into the library's gloom. It was built of dark wood and surrounded by leather chairs.

All but two chairs were empty. An Asian guy a little younger than me wearing wireless headphones tapped furiously at his laptop. He appeared to be so engrossed in whatever he was doing, he didn't look up.

I didn't pay the computer guy too much attention because of the ghost who sat across from him. Some ghosts can fool you. This one was obviously a misty wistful. He was an old man with a long white braid that reached to his waist. He appeared to be sleeping. I noticed those details later. The first thing I noticed was that I could see the chair *through* him. I hadn't seen so transparent a ghost before. His body was like a thin fog captured in a man-shaped glass mold.

Lesson 49: When you see something you haven't seen before and it's really weird and disturbing, your brain drops out for a moment, like a slipped gear. You blank out and it takes a minute to adjust.

All those movies where people meet an alien for the first time and they hardly react? Yeah, that's a bunch of crap. When the laws of the universe get rewritten before your eyes, take a minute to breathe deeply, down into your belly so you don't hyperventilate.

When the unexpected happens and it's so unexpected that it's beyond my capacity to be cool, sometimes it helps me to say, "This is really happening."

Of course, the rules of the universe were not rewritten before my eyes. The curtain was pulled back on how it really is.

"This is really happening," I said.

Imagine if your high school homeroom class suddenly reached up and all their faces were masks. Now imagine they all pulled their masks off at once and — *pop, pop!* — two rabbit ears emerged on each head and their faces were all rabbit faces with little pink bunny noses twitching. See that? Feel that? The shock of physics and facts changing fast is a little like that.

"There are more things in heaven and earth, Horatio, than are dreamt of in your philosophy." That was Victor. He must have been reading my face because, like I said, my mind was a blank for a few seconds.

"*Hamlet*," I said. "That's *Hamlet*." When the earth turns sideways, hold on to the anchors you trust to right yourself.

Victor came toward me, his arms out for a hug. "Another daughter joins the Choir."

I stiffened, but instead of hugging me, he took me by the shoulders and gave me a brisk, fatherly kiss on each cheek. Someday I hope to take the gesture gracefully. It's one of those European customs which will take this girl from rural Iowa a few years to get used to.

He stepped back and looked me up and down. "So, are you ready for your orientation? Do you know the origin of the term, the Choir Invisible?"

"It's from a George Eliot poem. It means 'the dead.'"

Victor's eyes widened in surprise.

"You ruined his, 'Welcome to the War' speech," Vlad

143

said.

"Vlad." Victor gave the big guy a look that meant *shut up*.

"Pity," Vlad said. "It *is* a good speech."

"I took it for granted that Iowa schools teach Shakespeare," Victor said. "I didn't know your poetics education would be so extensive."

"It's not." I held up my cell phone. "I checked my auxiliary brain. The Choir Invisible was either George Eliot or a reference to a Monty Python sketch. I took a shot."

Victor burst out laughing and the guy on the computer glanced up from his screen. His gaze slid over me as he checked me out. When he caught my look, he reddened and went back to his screen.

"So?" I asked. "Why George Eliot? Was he like you? A part-time poet and founder of a secret paramilitary organization for his day job?"

Victor grinned wider. "I guess you only had time to scan your google search. George Eliot was the pen name for a wonderful English novelist. Her real name was Mary Ann Evans."

"Okay. Why the Choir Invisible, though? For your... er...organization's name, I mean."

"An excellent question that gets to the root of our most honorable quest to save humanity."

"That's a line from the speech," Vlad whispered in my ear.

"The Choir Invisible," Victor continued, "does not simply mean, 'the dead.' When the author refers to the Choir Invisible, she speaks of living on past death through her words and deeds. The poem is a plea to be counted among," he quoted, "'those immortal dead who live again in minds made better by their presence.'"

"So she doesn't mean immortality like living forever? Like the way most people want it?"

"There are several kinds of immortality," Victor said. "If you aren't lucky enough to have been born a god, the next best is to live on through your benevolent actions. Each member of the Choir Invisible protects the secret of the Unseen and the structural integrity of the walls between worlds. If we live forever, it is likely only as heroes."

"Also from the speech," Vlad whispered to me.

"Got it, Vlad."

"In the Choir Invisible," Victor continued, "we strive for lasting heroics so our deaths will mean something. Our *legacy* is our immortality. We strive to live on that way, and not," — Victor gestured to the sleeping ghost — "that way."

I thought of all those sad-faced specters lined up outside the cemetery fence at Holy Cross. "Sounds like a good goal."

"It is the highest goal. All else is vanity."

The dead man sitting at the table stirred but did not open his eyes. I jumped a little in fright. "I remind you," he said, "I am here. And there, too, but I am listening." His accent was British. "Victor? How can a man as fussy about his clothes as you are dare to complain of others' vanity?"

"Sorry, old friend. Tamara? This is Rory. He is an ally."

I hadn't forgotten why I was there but it seemed everyone else had. "That's all fine, but tonight I'm worried about — "

145

"Dr. Carl Brooks," Rory said. "Born the bastard son of Todd Adams, nephew to Ada, who passed recently. Gone, but not forgotten."

"How did you know? Magic?"

"Sam called me," Victor said. It was his turn to hold up his cell phone and look smug.

The Asian guy pulled a headphone away from one ear and said shyly, "I found the house in Queens. The one where you saw the bodies. Once we had an address, I got the street view of the house on Google maps so Rory could zero in on Carl's evil emanations. I'm St. Charles, by the way. Before you ask, St. Charles is in Illinois." He smiled. "But I am quite saintly."

I turned to Vlad. "Okay…translation?"

"They are on it. Dr. Carl Brooks will not escape."

"Rory is our radar," St. Charles said.

"Radar that can't sense evil without a map?"

"There are too many evil emanations," the dead man explained. "It is more difficult than you can fathom, paying attention to only one bad person. We are surrounded by bad people. However, I do try to keep an eye on everything to make sure things do not get out of hand, or too close. For instance, how did you sleep last night, Tamara Smythe of Iowa? You looked like you slept well."

"What are you? Rory the Pervert Ghost?"

"He's joking," St. Charles said. "Rory's a Casper. He's a friendly ghost."

I looked to Vlad for confirmation. The big man nodded. "He is probably joking. With ghosts, it is harder to tell but my experience with Rory is that he is a gentleman."

"Well, that's just awesome."

"I assure you," Victor said, "you are precisely where you need to be and where you are needed. A great conflagration is coming and New York will be one of the first cities the enemy will attack."

"Okay," I said. Of course, none of this was okay. Sam had talked about "the big picture" and told me I "didn't know the half of it." I still felt like I was lost in the dark. "So, what's the plan to save the world from ghosts and serial killers?"

Everyone froze and Rory opened his eyes to look at me. (He opened the foggy wisps that passed for his eyelids, actually. Rory had no eyes, just black pits. Still, they were pointed my way so I assumed he could see me.)

"We aren't in a war with ghosts, Tamara," Vlad said. "Most move on and some don't. Some are good and some are bad, just as they were when they were alive and human."

I was losing patience. "You keep talking about the Choir Invisible as your army. Who's the enemy?"

"They go by many names," Victor said. "We call them the Darkness Visible."

I sighed. "Of course, you do."

Vlad bent to whisper in my ear. "Victor has a flair for the dramatic. Darkness Visible names the evil army trying to break through to our dimension from their hellscape dimension. They plan to take over the world and kill us all."

"Of course, they do." I couldn't help it. I did what Mama demanded I never do. I rolled my eyes.

"Also, you should know, The Darkness Visible has nothing to do with the book about depression by William

Styron," Vlad hastened to add. "That would be ridiculous."

I looked from Vlad to St. Charles to Victor and finally to Rory. "If we aren't busting ghosts, what are we doing?"

"There are several races trying to cross dimensions," St. Charles answered.

"They are alien to us, even to my kind," Rory said, "but we know they go by many names. Collectively, they call themselves the Ra. Their leader is Ba'al. When they have broken through the thin membrane between our world and theirs, Hell will return to Earth. It's been here before, it will happen again."

"Ra was beaten back long ago when magic was mankind's primary weapon. We can push them back and seal them off as we did before. We will find the right spells to cast, defend our world and divide the dimensions," Victor vowed.

"But the trouble is, a lot of that old knowledge has been lost," St. Charles said. "I'm trying to find answers in my research, but it's an uphill slog in slippery mud. I'm scanning the whole library online so we can find the solution again." He gestured to the library shelves. "The answer is there somewhere."

I turned to Vlad, who I knew now, would speak plainly. He did not disappoint. "For lack of a better word, Miss Tamara, we are fighting demons."

"*What?*" I said.

"Demons."

"*Demons from a Hell dimension?*"

"That is correct."

"And the Choir Invisible's job is to stop them from coming to New York, taking all our stuff and killing us?"

"More specifically," Victor said, "they want to *eat* us, but yes, that is our mission."

"Well…" I said, "sounds reasonable."

Rule 50: Don't laugh. It could happen to you.

# 24

"*Demons*? Really?"

"They may as well be," Victor said. "Call them aliens if it makes you feel better, but most of them certainly look like depictions of demons from the ancient scrolls and holy books. I know this is a lot to absorb, but please, come with me. I'd like to show you something more and we have much to discuss."

"What about the man who almost killed me tonight?" I asked.

Victor turned to the dead man. "Rory? An update, please?"

"Dr. Brooks doesn't want to go to jail, but he's not running because he doesn't want to lose his awful little house and his career. He's digging under the house, furiously. I'm sure he plans to hide the evidence of his sins. He'll be occupied for quite some time."

"We'll see justice done, Tamara," Victor said. "I promise."

As much as Vlad irritated me at first, I was nervous leaving the big guy's side. His capacity for telling painful truths might alert me if Victor strayed into a lie. However, I followed Victor out of the library and left Vlad with St. Charles and Rory.

Soon, Victor led me out of the library's gloom to a high catwalk that led to a tall stone wall. Victor's cane made a sharp metallic click every time he swung it. We walked along the top of the wall and, though it was dark, I guessed we were about four stories up. The wall was just wide enough for two people to stroll abreast. Shards of broken glass and crosses lined the brink.

"This is our bailey," Victor said. "It's the outer wall of our little castle. One of New York's first Roman Catholic churches once stood here and this rampart kept men out of the nunnery. That's the legend. I think it's true. It is our sanctuary from the war."

"No sentries on your castle wall?"

Victor looked pleased. "That's most unusual. People often see what's in front of them but few think to ask what is missing."

"I watch a lot of *Game of Thrones*."

"What's that?"

I thought of the armory and the Blade Room, stocked with so many swords. "It's a show on HBO. It's kind of like your life, Victor. You're just short one very short man and a lot of gratuitous nudity."

Victor used his cane to point to several security cameras as we passed them. The small cameras were tough to spot in the dark, hidden as they were in recessed pockets between stones.

"These are our sentinels. You'll find that, with security, we combine old and new magical practices, training and tactics. We have little to fear from demons here, at least for now. The coven reinforces the repelling spells each noon and midnight and whenever the moon is high and full. The enchantment shores up our defenses. Plus, this is holy ground. Keeps out most of the riffraff, except for Rory."

"How's that, sir?"

"He's never fully here. He's at your attacker's house and here, too. Quantum physicists put an atom in two places at once in 1996. Rory's been doing that feat for much longer. He's one of the oldest ghosts I've met. He claims he came over on the Mayflower. Nonsense, probably, but even Vlad isn't entirely sure when Rory's joking or boasting."

I thought again of the dead man teasing me, asking how well I slept. I made a vow to myself to wear the long flannel pajamas to bed from now on.

"I love our little castle," Victor said. "I didn't have much when I was a child so I became quite a hoarder. I always loved to stuff the wood box to overflowing and to stock up on groceries in case of a big storm."

"A storm's coming, huh?"

He nodded. "One of our seers predicts that one day there will be a great battle here and I will not survive it."

"That's dumb," I said, a little too fast to be respectful, but it had been a hard night and it didn't look like it was going to get softer.

"You don't believe in seers?" he asked. "The one who predicted my death is banned from gambling in any casino anywhere in North America. She's quite good."

"No, I mean that if you believe her, why aren't you on a beach in the south of France? If she can really predict the future, couldn't you avoid a lot of trouble and be somewhere else?"

"If we run from Death, Death will find us on the road to Damascus. Death must be met."

"Why?"

"From my reading, I'd say that's one of the few constants across dimensions."

"So if the demons break through to our dimension — "

"Some already have, a few at a time."

"And why isn't this on CNN?"

"The PTB want to keep this quiet."

"The who?"

"PTB. Powers That Be."

"Right. I knew that. Mama uses that phrase a lot, always around tax time."

"If we fail, the PTB are worried they won't collect tax anymore. I don't know what would cause more trouble," Victor said. "News that we can be trapped between dimensions after death or that demons are breaking through and coming for our blood."

"Sam filled me in. The fear seems to be that if everyone knows the truth, consumers would be less likely to relax and whip out a credit card at Best Buy."

"Yes. Essentially. When it comes to capitalism versus demonic invasion — "

"Bet on demons," I said.

He chuckled. "No sense soft pedaling it. You understand what's at stake."

"Riots in the streets."

"Things would look pretty grim unless you invested in evil demon futures."

"Isn't that what you've done here, Victor? This whole place looks to me like a big investment in demon futures."

"I suppose it is. I like to think I'm an optimistic person,

but the Keep suggests otherwise, doesn't it?"

"So why don't you leave this to the PTB? You have a lot of nice toys and all, but, with respect, isn't the power of the National Guard and Blackhawk helicopters going to be more to the point?"

Victor laughed. "Those tools might come into play if there's a big invasion, but I suspect that would be like bringing a Nerf bat to a knife fight. They do have a committee at the Pentagon in charge of the Development Group. They're working on the problem, I assure you. However, most of the PTB are working on the interdimensionality science. It's a tricky thing to discuss, even in closed meetings."

"Of course. Because it's all too insane."

"That is the PTB's weakness. Until they bring in a bunch of seers, witches, warlocks and monks, I don't think the government forces will be packing the right sort of staff when Doomsday comes."

"What's the Development Group?"

"Most people know them as Seal Team Six. They call themselves the Development Group."

I paused. In the dim light, I looked into the old man's eyes. I didn't need Vlad with me to confirm my intuition. It was obvious now. "Mr. Fuentes, you're a defense contractor."

His eyebrows shot high. Before he could lie, I warned him, "If I ask Vlad, he'll tell me."

"It's classified, but I will tell you the truth. Yes. A private interest such as ours gives the PTB plausible deniability if we lose operational security...or containment. How did you guess?"

"Until a couple of days ago, I've never heard of you. I

think it would take a billionaire to get this place going and run it. I'm sure you do very well, but a chain of funeral homes and an antiques shop couldn't fund this."

"Sadly true."

"Tell me how you propose we stop the Darkness Visible."

Victor looked eager. "The membranes between dimensions are a physical barrier, but they are also a *spiritual* barrier. We've learned a lot from watching ghosts to discern how to deal with the Ra. It's wrapped up in a lot of ancient magic that, frankly, I have a hard time picturing a bunch of young Marines wielding."

"Ghosts and demons exist on the same principles?"

"Not always, but the demons need to cross energy bridges to get here. Demons share the same environment as our dead but not gone. We've been studying the commonalities, looking for a chink in the Ra's armor. I'm convinced that, with the scrolls and books we've collected, we'll sort out the enemy's weaknesses."

"So sacred ground is something ghosts and demons don't like?"

"Most ghosts, except for Rory, of course, don't feel comfortable on holy ground. The demons hate it, though we've seen them tolerate it. Holy ground to them is like…"

"Playing death metal at full volume in a nursing home?"

"Excellent example."

I was thinking of Brad. "If a ghost is stuck here, how do we help them move on?"

"To kill a ghost, and by that I mean to make him or her move on to the next dimension, there are certainly things you can do. Those spirits who died in their sleep or through freezing, drowning or blood loss are sometimes nothing more than confused. They left this world but didn't go all the way into the next. They died confused, so we simply tell them they are dead. When they understand they are lost and not where they are supposed to be, they vanish. It's a beautiful way to help a lost spirit who doesn't belong here anymore."

"Wow, so I should get a megaphone and tell all those ghosts loitering outside Holy Cross that they're toast."

Victor shook his head. "If they are there, they already know they're dead. Those tormented souls are aware of their circumstance and they desperately want to leave. We don't understand why some of the dead stay. Ask Rory and he'll tell you he has no idea why he's still here. If a ghost is truly trapped here, we can only assume it's because the order of the multiverse deems them unsuitable for the next level."

"How else do you get a ghost to move on?"

"Bury a ghost in sacred ground, like a cemetery, and they're off to places unknown, far from here in the next dimension."

"How do you bury a ghost? I've never seen one lie down."

"Toss a shovelful of consecrated earth at them. That will do the job. It won't work if they are condemned to pine and moan outside a cemetery, though. Those spirits you saw outside of Holy Cross must be damned. Fortunately, the faces do change over time, so some of them move on. We must assume they all move on eventually. We see no caveman ghosts wandering around. Some of the people I saw around Holy Cross Cemetery when I was a kid of twenty aren't there anymore."

"Oh, my God."

"You'll mostly be concerned with battling demons," Victor said. "Regular bullets don't work on demons so well. You can annoy them and knock them down, but they often get back up and keep coming. We figured it out after losing some good people. To take down demons with guns, each round must be blessed individually. It's a very time-consuming process."

"I saw lots of guns in the Keep's armory."

"It's not just demons who may choose to stand against us. I believe you found that out tonight with Dr. Brooks."

"I don't follow."

"Ghosts used to be human, Tamara. As Vlad said, they can be as good or as bad as anyone. I think the boredom of their in-between existence drives many of them crazy. Bad ghosts used to be bad humans."

"You're talking about shooting humans, though, aren't you? When Armageddon comes."

"Didn't you tell Sam to shoot a human just this evening?"

"I did. I only did it because I didn't think I had any choice."

"Everything we must face is against our will. Believe me, I'd prefer to deal with more mundane problems than the end of the world. I should be retired and publishing poetry, not readying for a war."

"I might have issues with killing humans. Tell me about the demons. That sounds like a video game I can get behind."

"The demons are so desperate to get out of Ra, they're often like rabid dogs when they find their way to us. For them, you'll need a sword. "

"Swords? Like *Highlander*? Do you have to cut their heads off to kill them?"

"Any vital organ will do, though beheading is remarkably effective on all species we've encountered. However, only *blessed* steel works."

"Blessed. How do we know this?"

"We have a copy of a scroll that is, at this moment, sitting in a vault under the Vatican. We tested the hypothesis. Blessed blades kill demons efficiently."

"Is the Choir Invisible a cult? Do I have to sell flowers at the airport for a while before I go up a level in the pyramid or something?"

Victor smiled and shook his head. "The blessings of many religions will do. Almost everything seems to work as long as there is faith behind it."

"Interesting. Mama will be pleased. She admits she's not a very good Presbyterian, but once I tell her all this, I'm sure she'll say a prayer over her cleaver and the steak knives."

Victor looked out over the city lights. He appeared to sober at the mention of my mother. "Well, Tamara, this is where we get to the uncomfortable part of the evening."

"Is it going to be worse than a serial killer holding a scalpel to my throat?"

"Possibly. It's about your mother."

"You don't want me to tell her."

"No, no. You can tell her. She already knows."

Lesson 51: To survive Armageddon, don't trust what you think you know.

# 25

"How could my mother know anything about this? When I told her I could see my dead boyfriend, she sent me to a mental hospital. Do you know what happened to me?"

"Yes. I know. I've spoken with your mother."

That brought me to a dead stop and left me gasping. "Wh-what?"

"You're the last to know, I'm afraid. Before we continue, I must ask you two questions. First, why haven't you tried to see your father?"

I blinked back tears. "I don't even remember him. I've been putting it off, trying to find an apartment and a job and…I just…I don't know."

"Did you want to avoid disappointment, perhaps?"

"I just wanted to get myself together before I opened up to meeting him. I didn't want my father to think I wanted anything. He left when I was young. If I needed any help and he gave it, that would make what he did okay. Who leaves a wife and baby?"

"Warriors," Victor said. "In cases of war, many warriors must leave their loved ones behind in order to protect them. Even when...*especially* when those they leave behind are too young to defend themselves."

Before I could argue, he raised a hand. "But I think I understand your position. I just understand Peter Smythe's position, too."

"Good for you. I don't."

That was the first I'd heard my father's name spoken aloud in years. Of course, I knew his name. I'd spoken it aloud to myself many times, usually as a little girl standing at my window hoping my father would finally come home. I never spoke his name aloud within Mama's earshot.

If she had to refer to her former husband, she'd say, "your father," or, "that man." As in, "That man left us with a ton of bills. I'll be paying them off forever."

"Please," Victor said, bringing me back to the present, "Come with me. I have something to show you. There are four buildings in the complex. You have toured three: the armory, the greenhouse and the library. The fourth begins at the far end of this wall. It is the barracks and the clinic."

We turned left into another building. From the outside, it looked like just another warehouse, hulking, black and windowless. Like the others, it was as long as a city block.

"To house our army," Victor said. The layout reminded me of a dormitory. It probably wasn't much different from the university dorm rooms I should have been attending that fall.

"What does this have to do with my father?" I asked.

Victor appeared to be choosing his words carefully. "Before there was a barracks or a greenhouse, your father started the library. He had visions, just as you have had."

"Mama said it was schizophrenia."

"I have found several of our strongest warriors in mental hospitals, Tamara."

"If she knew my father wasn't crazy, why did she say he was? How could Mama put me in a mental hospital if she knew the truth?"

Then I remembered what she said as she left me at Shibboleth. *I don't want to leave you here...but it's the right thing to do. I want you cured, okay? I want you safe. I love you so much, baby girl.*

I cried then. It wasn't the kind of crying where silent tears slide down your face and you get to preserve a little dignity. I cried big, hot baby tears and I snuffled a lot. My nose ran and I wiped it away with my forearm. Victor offered me a handkerchief.

"Don't be too hard on your mother. Ellen wants to keep you out of the war."

"Ellen? You know her? Do you know her well? Like Sam?"

For a moment I wondered if Victor was about to confess that he was my father. "That day at Holy Cross, did you follow me? That couldn't have been a chance meeting! Are you my father?"

"No." Victor wiped away my tears. "I do wish I was, though. Your father would have been very proud of you. Ellen raised a smart and strong daughter. And yes," he said, "I got you to come to me."

"How?"

He shook his head. "It matters little, but it was a small charm, a stone actually. It has old magic. One of our seekers found it on the bottom of the Sea of Mull in Scotland. I had it with me that day. When I looked at you through the stone, you were drawn to me."

"My God! You roofied me! You magic roofied me!"

"I wouldn't put it that way."

"How would you put it?"

"Er...*another* way." He looked flustered. "Your mother tried to protect you, but denying your talents is denying the inevitable. You're safer among warriors now. You're part of this. You're one of us. You belong with the Choir."

"I could walk away."

"Doubtful," he said.

"Why not?"

"Because you have genetic gifts that could help us win this war. If we lose to the demons, you'll be in the war, anyway. Everyone and everything you have ever loved will be in the war. I'll give you a hint. They are demons. They don't have mercy."

Everything I ever loved would be in danger except the one person who mattered most now. Brad was safe from Armageddon. He could only have his arms ripped off and bleed to death once.

I stared at Victor, trying to process all he'd said. Ghosts and demons were real. Magic was real. Magic had fallen out of fashion, but it had been around a lot longer than science and now magic was making a comeback.

Victor and I stopped at a glassed-in catwalk high above a courtyard. I realized now that the four buildings of the complex formed a massive rectangle. When I went up on tip toes, I could see three courtyards. Two great stone walls cut through the center so the area in the middle was divided in thirds. I could make out the ruins of a church spire at the far end of the courtyard to my left.

The parapet I'd walked atop was visible behind the library and the church ruins. I hadn't understood how big the Choir Invisible's stronghold really was until now.

The high walls inside the Keep's courtyards were not constructed of wood and black metal as they had been on the outside facing the streets. Each wall that rose from the courtyards was made of stone.

In the center of each courtyard, young men and women in what looked like chain mail practiced with swords and spears and bows and arrows. Most of the swords were made of wood, but not all. I could hear metal ring on metal here and there as the Choir Invisible practiced. It looked like a scene from a movie.

"The stones that line the courtyard walls are from ancient, destroyed churches from all over the world," Victor said. "Quartzite, metamorphic rock, ordovician dolostone...even some coral."

I glanced back at the ruins of the church crumbling by the far wall. "Didn't seem to help that church much."

"That collapsed from decay. This is strategy. The vibrations of millions of worshipers contemplating a blissful life eternal are trapped in those stones. The Corps of Monks say so, anyway. We look for any advantage over the demons. Those walls burn and repel the Darkness Visible."

I tore my gaze away from the sparring below. "Then why didn't you put all that stone to good use on the *outside* walls?"

Victor smirked. "We didn't want to attract undue attention. Just making sure our little piece of Brooklyn is a no-fly zone costs millions each year. More important, this courtyard is a trap. The same battle that takes me will, I hope, trap the invasion force and end the war."

"I'm supposed to be blown away, huh?"

"You're not impressed by the Keep?"

"Sorry, it's just a bit much to take in all at once. Mama and I are going to have to have a serious talk about honesty. She freaked out when I lied about brushing my teeth at bedtime once. Her lies almost got me killed at Shibboleth."

"She was lying to herself as much as to you," Victor said. "She didn't want you to follow your father's path."

"Looks like I am on his path now, doesn't it? Besides, I really want to try on that chain mail. I'd look hot in chain mail."

Victor laughed, but he shut up when I shot him what Mama called, "the hairy eyeball."

"You haven't told me where to find my father. Don't you think it's time you stopped talking around it?"

"Peter Smythe is buried in the courtyard down there, at the foot of the wall. He died bravely. A demon named Cord, little brother to and bodyguard of Ra's King Ba'al, killed him with a spear."

"When?"

"Last spring."

"I see."

Victor put a light hand on my shoulder. "Are you okay?"

"I'm feeling a little more sympathy for my mother all of a sudden," I said.

"And about your father?"

"He's already been dead a long time. To me, anyway. Where is Cord now?"

Victor gestured to our view of the skyline beyond the Keep. "Here or back in Ra. He is one of those few who seem to be able to cross the barrier between dimensions with more ease. I have seen him. He often occupies the Ghost's in-between dimension. I'm sorry. We have been unable to avenge Peter's death."

"Where does this leave me?"

"Here. Now."

I looked for a marker above my father's grave but I couldn't see it from where I stood on the catwalk.

After a time, Victor cleared his throat. "People have forgotten what war is. We send a few dedicated people far away and the view most people get of what is done is sanitized. War touched us on 9/11. When the Darkness Visible breaks through, war will come again to New York and they'll come to stay."

"How soon?"

"We're using strong enchantments to keep them out. No large force has broken through yet, but some demons get through, one or two at a time."

"So you don't know when the attack will come?"

"It could be in a month or a year. For now, it's our magic against theirs. Across the world, there are monasteries of all stripes. The monks and nuns chant just as their orders have prayed for thousands of years. Whenever anyone says the words, 'deliver us from evil,' it reinforces the wall between our dimension and Ra. Still, that barrier is weakening. They have powerful magic on their side, too."

Farther down the catwalk, Victor showed me a better view of the central courtyard. Below us, the swordplay went on. Most of the duels took place on circular pads. The pads formed concentric circles that reminded me of crop circles. This was the Choir Invisible's training ground.

I watched as two combatants slashed at each other with sabers. They were a girl and a boy, a little younger than me. The boy had an excellent parry. Each time the girl lunged at him, he knocked her blade aside. He even managed to knock the sword from her hand several times in a row. Every time she dropped her sword, he allowed her to pick it up and try again.

Mr. Chang would not have approved. "If you fail without consequence, you will repeat the mistake." Every time I tried to throw Mr. Chang and failed, he would throw me.

I looked at Victor. "You have a good defense. You can delay your opponents' victory with a good defense, but you will never win that way. The fighter who hits hard has an advantage. The fighter who hits fast has an advantage. The fighter who hits first can win over the hard and the fast. A good offense is the only defense that lasts."

That's Lesson 52.

"Do you wish to visit your father's grave and meet some of your compatriots?"

I hadn't seen my father since I was very young. Looking at the patch of grass that hid him away could wait.

"I don't know demons, sir." I said. "But there is a doctor in Queens who is a homicidal maniac. I can identify him. We should go get Brooks."

"Is that a yes to joining the Choir Invisible?"

"Like Mama says, let's eat what's on our plate first before we figure out if we have room for dessert."

# 26

Vlad drove Victor and me to Queens in an old VW bus. A young man and woman sat at the back of the bus. They might have been twenty-five or so.

The guy wore his hair long and loose and was dressed in black leather from head to toe. He carried a long walking staff. He wore one of those perpetual three-day beards that seem meticulously trimmed to look casually macho.

The woman was one of those glamor girls with smooth mocha skin and, to the naked eye, it appeared she had no pores. It was as if a photoshopped model had stepped out of a fashion magazine cover in thigh-high boots. She wore big glasses with heavy black frames. Her hair was coiled in a tight bun and a long string of pearls hung over a plunging neckline. Her dress was black with a subtle flower print. The weirdest thing was she carried a white parasol with a golden fringe.

I glanced back at them and asked Victor, "What's with young Gandalf and the sexy librarian?"

"Two of my best singers," Victor said.

I snorted, covered up, then burst into a laugh again. When I could control myself, I leaned forward to whisper to Victor. "If you people want to keep a low profile, I suggest you dress down. Nobody would notice an army of hipsters moving through the streets of New York. Give them all a Starbucks coffee to carry around and they'll blend in. I looked at those two for three seconds and could pick them out of any police line up."

"Noted." Victor smiled. "Thank you, Tamara."

Vlad, hunkered over the wheel, grunted. "That means he will not follow your suggestion, Miss Tamara."

"Thanks, Vlad. I got that. What's the plan, sir? Find Dr. Carl Brooks in a compromising position and call the cops?"

"Something like that."

I looked to Vlad. He shook his head. "Nothing like that."

Victor leaned closer to me. "You saw what Carl Brooks did when you channeled the dead woman?"

"That was channeling?"

"Yes."

"I wish I could change the channel. I didn't expect to throw up at the end of the vision." If I closed my eyes, I could still see the faces of those dead girls. Without teeth, their faces looked a third shorter than they should have been.

"And you understand that Rory saw what Dr. Brooks is doing?"

I nodded.

"Would you say Dr. Brooks is guilty?"

"Sure, I would."

"Just so," Victor said. "And would you agree that the

doctor is evil?"

Vlad interrupted before I could speak. "It is possible there is not Evil with a big *E*. Actions can be evil. Perhaps the doctor is simply mentally ill in a dangerous way. This is an important distinction."

Victor sighed. "Making fine distinctions is how we will lose this war. Would you agree, Vlad, that the doctor's *actions* are Evil, with a big *E*, whether he is personally evil or deranged?"

Vlad nodded.

"Then his actions are weakening the wall between us and the armies of the Darkness Visible." Victor raised his voice so the pair at the back of the bus could hear him. He was not simply answering my question anymore. He was giving a speech. "Every act of evil counters the energy of a thousand prayers. The activities of every individual throughout the realms of the multiverse echo and impact the dynamics of the world that person inhabits. Our actions also affect the structural integrity of the barriers between dimensions. By executing the guilty, our objective tonight is to stop not only the man, but to stop Hell itself from spilling over into our world. To strengthen the wall, it is insufficient to bring Carl Brooks to justice in our world. If he was to travel the long journey through the justice system's machine, his emanations would still contribute to weakening the wall that keeps the Ra at bay. Brooks must be erased. Everything we think and do lends energy to or pulls energy from the architecture of the universe. This is a psychic war as much as it is a physical one."

My jaw dropped. If she'd been there, Mama would have said, "Close your mouth, Tammy. You're catching flies."

His speech reminded me of Samantha's words about the value of working at the funeral home. "This is a valuable opportunity to serve people when our service is most needed." Sam was helping to keep the barrier against the demons strong, too. Despite wanting to opt out and pretend the world was more peaceful than it was, Sam was a warrior in her own way. She was a warrior in a way I preferred. Being nice to people and performing a random act of kindness each day sounded like an easier path than slaying demons.

Finally, I found my voice. "Victor, you're talking about murder."

"I'm talking about saving lives."

I looked to Vlad. He said nothing. My living lie detector kept his eyes on the road.

"War has different rules, Tamara," Victor said. "We are on the side of the angels."

Vlad cleared his throat and Victor jumped in, "*Metaphorical* angels, Vlad! It's an idiom. I mean, of course, we're doing what we must to stave off Armageddon. To keep the Darkness Visible out, we must slay the Darkness *Invisible* that's already inside our borders."

"This is nuts," I said. "You better let me out here." I had no idea where I was, but I felt like I was in the wrong place with crazy people. If Sam could opt out, so could I. I'd keep my head down and be nice to grieving people and maybe chant, *"Deliver us from evil,"* a few times a day.

"How long until we get to our objective?" Victor asked.

"A few minutes more," Vlad said, "depending on traffic and depending where Miss Tamara would like us to drop her off. Statistically, this is not a good neighborhood in the pre-dawn hours."

Victor turned in his seat to face me. His tone was desperate. "George Sand said, 'the artist's vocation is to send light into the human heart.' The Choir Invisible protects that light."

"George who?"

"She was a French novelist," Victor said.

"What is it with you and women named George?"

"My point is, if we do our duty and stay true to the warrior's vocation, that light will remain unsullied."

I gave him a blank stare. I was already part of a conspiracy to murder. It was worse every minute I stayed on the bus. "Please, just call the police. Let them handle Carl Brooks. I believe in killing in self-defense. Believe me, I do! But going to his house where the bodies are buried... that's different."

Victor took my hand. "Tamara. A while ago I heard an old man, a veteran of World War II, talking about how young people today don't know what he went through. 'They don't know and they don't care.' The old fellow was pretty worked up about it. I told him that the innocence of children, ignorant of war, is what he fought for. We do our work in secret so that, when it's all over, we will still recognize the Earth we fought for. The human race's innocence must be preserved. If we involve the police, our little house of cards will fall."

I didn't know what to say. But I didn't insist Vlad pull over and let me out, either.

Lesson 53: Refusing to make a choice is still making a choice.

I felt a cool hand on my shoulder. It was the sexy

librarian. "You say you believe in killing in self-defense."

"Yes. When necessary — "

"This is necessary. It's not just you that you are defending. You're defending everyone, everywhere."

I gave the slightest nod of assent, but it was enough to commit and convict me.

Lesson 54: With a lot of choices, once you make them, there's no way back.

Lesson 55: If you're a girl, don't call yourself George and don't name your daughter George. That's just mean.

# 27

The house in Queens was not what I expected. I expected the serial killer cliche: a small, shabby ruin. Instead, it was a large house set back from the road. The lawn was freshly trimmed and a colorful flower box hung beneath each window. I guess that's how bad guys blend in.

Lesson 56: If that makes you a little paranoid about your neighbors (who all seem to lead such quiet and nice lives), you're on the right track.

Vlad parked the minibus across the street and a few doors down. We watched the house for movement. The garage door was closed and the lights were out. It looked like no one was home.

Victor called St. Charles on his cell. "Is he still in the house?"

St. Charles's voice came through the speaker. "Rory says he's in the basement. He's not alone, but Rory can't say who's with him."

The others glanced at each other and the tension in their jaws ratcheted up. They were not pleased that Brooks was with someone Rory couldn't identify.

"Closest PTB?" Victor asked.

We heard Charles tap on his keyboard. "Closest duty cops are seven away. Huge build up of police activity far from you. Some crazy idiot Swatted somebody."

"Good job, St. Charles." Victor hung up.

"What's 'Swatted' mean?" I asked.

The beautiful girl with perfect skin answered. "We got the idea from hoax calls on celebrity homes. Somebody called police to say there was a man with a gun firing shots in Clint Eastwood's mansion. Something like that. Anyways, naturally, the police sent SWAT and everybody else on duty wanted in on that action, too. They all wanted to claim to save Dirty Harry's life, maybe get a picture with Clint himself."

"It's effective in drawing away the PTB," Victor said.

"Sounds dangerous," I said.

"It is," the girl agreed. "It's an incredibly dumb thing to do that can get people killed, unless you're us. We use Rory to zero in on known felons and their evil emanations. St. Charles supplies the mugshots so Rory can find them more easily. The cops have already taken down three guys of the FBI's top ten list of fugitives thanks to us. But does the FBI send flowers? No."

I laughed. "Cool."

"I'm Manhattan," the sexy librarian said. "The guy with the stick is Bronx, not Gandalf. We heard you talking about us."

My cheeks got hot, but I was too curious not to ask about their names.

"The name I was born with was Poala," she said, "but when you join the Choir, the tradition is that you take the name of the home you fight for."

"What if two of you are from one place?"

She shrugged. "We can work it out peacefully or you can fight for your name. Some people just get more specific. We've got a Jackson from Jackson Heights, a Gramercy, a Greenwich and the girl named Chelsea is actually from Chelsea."

"Good news. Chelsea sure lucked out, huh?" I said.

Her eyes narrowed and she pursed her lips. "We're proud to serve and we've seen things you can only imagine. Where you from, White Bread?"

"Iowa."

"Good news," she said. "If you join up, you won't have to fight for that name."

"Well, you know, Manhattan," I began, "the thing about Iowa is — "

"No one cares!"

"That's what I was going to say," I deadpanned.

Vlad turned in his seat and was about to call me on my lie, I'm sure. I put up a palm like a stop sign. "Don't even!"

Bronx came forward and I thought he was about to shake my hand. Instead, he asked gruffly, "You're not a soprano yet, but we can't let you go in without something. Umbrella or cane?"

"What?"

"Umbrella, it is." He shoved a dainty little parasol into my hands. "For your protection, White Bread."

I looked down at the parasol. It looked like a child's umbrella from another century (one of the way back ones.)

Vlad reached from the driver's seat and twisted the parasol's handle counterclockwise. A shiny blade popped into view. I drew it out and looked at the blade. It was a long triangular knife and surprisingly heavy. Each edge was sharp and, close to the hilt where the blade was thickest, it became a cruel saw with steel teeth.

"I've never seen a knife like this at Walmart."

"It's not just a knife," Manhattan said. "It's a dirk. The edges can cut viciously. The triangular blade opens a wound that does not close to hasten bleeding. You can cut and slice with it or thrust, too, for maximum damage. Serrated is good."

I stared at her a moment. I felt like a poster of a bloodthirsty eyeglasses model had come to life to lecture me on knife technology. "Thanks?" I said.

"Don't worry," Vlad added. "I blessed the blade myself during its making. It's best that way."

"*You* blessed it?"

He shrugged. "I am a priest."

"Oh." I wondered what order of priests also trained in MMA and lifted weights all day. Stuffed tightly into his suit, Vlad looked like he was ordained in the Holy Order of Kick Ass.

Manhattan put her hand on the side door. "You ready to rock, farm girl? Stay behind us. You're here as an observer. If you see Brooks, be sure to let us know. We'll handle it and you won't have to get your hands dirty."

"Yeah," Bronx added. "Eyes open, mouth shut."

"Manhattan. Bronx," Victor said, "play nice. She's a legacy candidate."

"I am?"

Vlad looked to Victor. "Boss? You should drive the getaway bus. I'll guard the girl this time."

Victor nodded and slid into the driver's seat as Vlad got

out. The big Russian took his umbrella with him, winked at me and looked up at the sky. He held his palm up as if feeling for raindrops. "Just in case, Miss Tamara."

"I *tink* you are a *leetle* funny," I said. I noticed his umbrella was much bigger than mine and I wondered what the hidden blade looked like. "I guess that's a better solution than running around New York City with a long sword crammed under your armpit and trying to hide it with a trench coat all the time."

"Let's go!" Manhattan said.

I was about to ask what the plan was, but she and Bronx were already making their way across the street. They headed straight for the house of the man who had threatened to decapitate me. (I had mixed feelings about it, but mostly, I felt terror.)

Once the singers were close to the house, they both broke into a run. Bronx went around to the back while Manhattan peered in the windows. I followed Vlad. Given the width of his shoulders, from behind, Vlad looked like a triangle. I made a mental note to tell him to work on his calves more. Still, it felt like I was walking behind a shield of meat and muscle.

That wouldn't help much if Brooks had a gun and started shooting. I was about to point that out when Vlad pulled a pistol from a shoulder holster. Then I noticed Manhattan had a small silver automatic. I was relieved the entire strategy for their raid wasn't based on medieval weapon technology.

Bronx must have found a way in through the back because he quietly opened the front door for us. He put a finger to his lips and pointed down. Bronx was not wearing his boots. His socks had holes in them.

177

I was about to step inside when Vlad stopped me and pointed to my shoes. Vlad slipped off his dress shoes. Manhattan put a hand on my shoulder for balance as she removed her boots.

When I looked up from slipping off my shoes, Vlad's umbrella had transformed into a sword. At first, I thought that was some kind of magic, like a magician's wand that turned into a bouquet of flowers. The truth was boring. The umbrella sheath to his sword lay in the grass by the step.

Vlad's blade caught the light and its edge glowed with a blue sheen. The steel by the hilt was etched with black butterflies spiraling up the blade. Along the last third of its length was a red dragon spouting fire. As soon as I saw it, I wanted one. No, I *coveted* Vlad's sword. I didn't know why, though his weapon would be a big improvement on the dinky blade they'd given me.

Once we all had our footwear off, Bronx pointed down again. Apparently, Brooks was still in the basement. As we entered the foyer, we stopped to listen. Staccato curses rose up through the floorboards.

Bronx beckoned us to follow him and we did. I brought up the rear, holding the blade with the sharp end pointed at the floor because Mama taught me not to run with scissors.

The entrance to the basement was in the kitchen. As soon as I got to the head of the stairs I began to sweat and my breathing became shallow. I forced myself to breathe into my belly to slow my hammering heart.

Rory waited for us on the landing. He looked less misty and more substantial than he had in the library. His eyes were open here. When the dead man looked at me, his eyes burned with bright orange flames. He pointed down the stairs in the direction of the constant flow of ragged curses.

My heart beat faster again and I really wanted to pee. Worse, my palms were sweaty and my short sword hilt was slippery in my fist. If not for the little gold pommel, I might have dropped my weapon.

Lesson 57: Dying makes you drop things. Get yourself a sword with rubber or rope grips so you won't drop it. Rubber grips on pistols make sense, too. You'll want to think you're so brave in the face of death that your palms won't sweat. But it's not death that will scare you in the end.

When the battle is lost, you'll embrace death and be grateful. It's all the stuff that happens just before death rescues you — the exquisite pain of shattered bones and torn muscles and nerves — that will make your palms sweaty.

# 28

When I passed Rory, my sweat froze on my face and I twitched as a shiver went up my spine. The dead man smiled at me and, for a moment, I was lost in his blazing eyes. I was careful not to touch the ghost, but in the small turn of the landing, I was close enough to feel his power.

Rory was unlike other ghosts I'd seen. A certainty came to me that I could not explain. Rory wanted to be here. The other souls caught between this world and the next were sad ghosts who were trapped by circumstances they did not understand. Rory had a sense of purpose working with the Choir Invisible.

On impulse, I waved my hand through the fog that was his right wrist. Dozens of images hit me in a flash: a stone hut with a thatch roof, a herd of sheep, a tall ship with three masts. The sun slowly sank into the ocean as I watched from atop the highest mast as the ship rolled and lunged beneath me in a high wind. I heard women and children laughing. That was the good part.

Then I looked up into Rory's blazing eyes and, through the fire, I sensed the evil in the world. I could feel the evil emanation of Brooks in the next room. I felt the presence of dozens of others nearby, too. They were all dangerous and I felt a new urge I had not felt since Shibboleth Mental Hospital. I wanted to stop them and the only way to do that was to kill them.

Lesson 58: Evil is a bleak, black thing you sense more than see. When you encounter the real thing, it feels like a knife at your throat. It smells of olives and feels like old oily rags sliding over your skin. It makes your skin hot and every hair on your body stands up, tingling and burning at the same time. Evil feels like it might spread easily, like a terrifying infection.

What I sensed through Rory ignited a rage I didn't know I was capable of. Evil invited me to become evil, to be just as savage in the cause of eliminating evil. I didn't know if I'd end up adding to the bad in the world or eradicating it. Yes, it was all very Luke Skywalker versus Darth Vader.

What alarmed me most was how much evil there was. I felt like I was nothing more than weak starlight trying to reach into the dark void between the stars. The hopelessness was overwhelming.

Then Rory spoke to me, though I was sure no one else could hear him. "Hopelessness and evil are wound tight together and make a lethal force that cares nothing for anyone. Don't give in to hopelessness, lass."

I squeezed my eyes tight and pulled away and I began to fall. Vlad caught me before I hit the floor.

I heard Rory whisper, "Not pretty is it? The battle must be joined. But now's not the time to get philosophical, love. For all the good talking does, it's hardly ever time to talk philosophy."

The dead man said something that sounded like Mr. Chang, "No matter what, put up a good fight. The enemy may win, but leave them bloody so they know they were in a fracas."

The visions slipped away, the dizziness passed and I got my feet under me. When I looked up, I realized Manhattan was staring at me. She held Bronx back from advancing deeper into the basement. Embarrassment made my cheeks and scalp hot and I gave her a nod to let her know we should continue.

Manhattan rolled her eyes. If we weren't trying to sneak up on Brooks, I would have taken the time to call her a bitch. She wasn't wrong, though, and Rory was right. Now was not the time for visions and debates. I'd committed to action once I crossed the threshold to this death house.

The first basement room was a small rec room with a couch pointed at an old television. The carpet was a dirty, dull orange, but it still had enough padding left to cover the sound of our approach.

I heard the sound of a shovel chunking into packed dirt. Bronx pressed a button in his staff. A spearhead emerged from each end of the weapon.

Bronx used his spear to carefully pull back the edge of a heavy brown curtain. At first, he only pulled it back an inch to peer into the gloom beyond the door frame. Satisfied it was safe, Bronx pulled the curtain back another inch…then another and another.

When I craned my neck, I could glimpse Brooks. I was relieved to see his back was to us as he went about his grim task, digging deeper under the dirt floor.

A large bag lay on the floor behind him. At first, I didn't know what I was looking at. Looking closer, I realized it was a thin, twisted hand covered in filth. No. Some of the bones of the hand were bare. Flesh doesn't last. Hair does. I saw a fall of long, matted hair at the edge of the bag.

Bronx held up three fingers. Then two. Then he rushed into the room where Brooks dug. He ran into the blade of a battle ax swung by a demon.

I only got a glimpse of the thing behind the curtain before it rushed at us. It was tall and it stood on two legs. There, the similarities between humans and demons pretty much ended. I couldn't tell if the black thing that had struck from the dark was covered in scales or if that was armor.

One moment, Bronx could have been an underwear model starring in a movie. The next, he was dead. His head rolled to my feet. His eyes stared up at me.

Manhattan, screaming in grief and fury, attacked. She raised her gun and shot through the curtain first, emptying her weapon quickly.

We heard a scream and, just as Manhattan came to the curtain, Brooks barreled out, knocking the girl to one side. The doctor's white shirt blossomed with two red wounds at his belly but he held his throat with both hands. One of Manhattan's wild shots had caught his neck. His tongue stuck out to one side. His eyes were wild. Brooks looked like he was trying to strangle himself as he attempted to stanch the rush of pumping blood.

I heard the sweep of Vlad's blade cut the air. The steel decorated with butterflies and dragons sliced through the top of Carl Brooks's head just above the eyes. He fell at my feet next to the spot where Bronx's head had rolled to a rest.

The demon came next. Manhattan must have slowed him with her pistol, but he came roaring through the door now with speed I wouldn't have expected from such a large creature. All it wore was a loin cloth, but its features were so alien, I didn't assume it was male.

I also didn't expect the horns. There were two, both on one side of the thing's head. They grew out raggedly at right angles.

I heard Rory scream, "Run, child!" At that moment, my knees were shaking under me. I doubt I could have run in that moment.

The monster knocked Vlad to my right before my bodyguard could swing his weapon again. It pulled back its double-headed battle ax. If not for the small space, I might have been killed. The ax blade bit deep into the wood of a low hanging rafter and held fast there a moment.

The demon roared, planted its feet wide and pulled its weapon free. It was too late to run. I dove forward between the monster's legs. Holding my short blade with one hand, I thrust the tip straight up, screaming and crying as I sat up, twisting the serrated blade.

The demon was a boy.

Then he was not. When a bad guy gets his junk cut off, I like to think it gives him pause to reevaluate his life choices.

Lesson 59: A demon's scream sounds like fingernails on chalkboard combined with a wolf howl. No matter what dimension you're from, the principle of pain is universal. No realm we know of escapes pain.

# 29

**V**lad lunged and thrust the tip of his sword under the creature's armpit and into its chest, searching for the heart (if the monster had a heart where humans keep theirs, anyway). But it was Manhattan's blade that made the decisive cut. She jumped on the demon's back, yanked its head back by its horns and sliced his throat open.

Black blood showered me like hot rain. Spitting, I crawled out of the way just in time, before I could be crushed under the thing's weight. The demon sank to his knees and tumbled backward.

Vlad bent to hold my hair out of the way as I threw up. I continued to vomit until there was nothing more left to give. It was the second time I'd puked that night. At least this time I didn't splash anything inside a dead woman's casket.

"Rory," Vlad said. "Please relay to St. Charles that we need a cleanup crew now."

The ghost nodded. "The monks are already on their way."

I stayed on my hands and knees, panting. "Cleanup?"

"When the police find Brooks," Vlad said, "there will be no trace of us or the supernatural. The PTB pays a lot of attention to murder scenes, but they won't find a giant demon when they investigate."

"The cleaners are very good, indeed," Rory said. "They are among the most secretive of the Choir's sects. If humans knew their magic spells for making dead bodies disappear, the world would be a much more dangerous place than it already is."

When I was ready, Vlad helped me to my feet.

"You fared well, Iowa," Rory said.

"I don't think it went so well," Manhattan said. She was on her knees, staring at Bronx's head and crying.

Bronx had been a handsome young man and now, with one stroke of incredible violence, he was gone.

I didn't think of Brad then. That might have been the first moment since his death that Brad was far from my thoughts. I thought a lot about my beautiful farm boy boyfriend afterward, though.

It seemed to me Bronx's death was an easier end. He didn't have time to contemplate what might come next. If he felt anything, it must have been surprise more than pain. Brad had to kick down his door, take a pencil in his mouth and try to make phone calls while his blood spilled everywhere. Bronx died a warrior. Brad died a victim. It might have been that moment that I decided to join the Choir Invisible. I vowed then to embrace the edict that I leave something behind that would last. Something good.

Or, in truth, maybe I decided to join when I realized it was in my self-interest to join the war against the demons.

"This was no happenstance," Rory said. "They killed the girl's father and now they hoped to kill her."

"Me?"

"You," Vlad said.

"Why?"

"Strategy," Manhattan said, never taking her eyes off Bronx's head. "By making it personal, they hope to bring down our morale and weaken our mission. If the Choir knows it's personal, we might even lose some singers."

"Ra sent a battle demon in full armor," Rory said. "They don't usually make it through the barrier. The last time was Peter Smythe's killer. And *this* demon hooked up with the serial killer. It wouldn't surprise me if Dr. Brooks murdered Ada Adams somehow, poison maybe. He was a doctor. He'd know how. Then they chose the funeral home carefully — "

"Hold on," I said, "...you're saying demons and humans *worked together to kill me?*"

"This was a trap," Vlad said. "When Rory couldn't identify the other person with Brooks, we suspected this might be the case."

I whirled on Vlad. "You suspected but you still brought me down here?"

"Either, or," Vlad said, "what would we have done differently?"

I stared. "You said you were my bodyguard. The cautious thing to do would be to keep me out of it. If your enemy wants you to do something, don't do it!"

Manhattan stood. "We're the Choir, White Bread. We don't do cautious. We slay evil. You wanna be safe? Slay evil. Or go back to Iowa and wait for the demons to find you there."

That's when it occurred to me that maybe the demons already had found me in Iowa. Maybe Brad's death wasn't a stupid accident. Maybe it was a stupid murder. If I wasn't Peter Smythe's daughter, a legacy candidate, Brad might still be alive.

I cried. I cried until dawn crept over New York City. As the dark receded and the grays and shadows pulled back to be replaced with color, I swore I'd stop crying and start doing.

That's Lesson 60. Stop crying and start doing.

Before I shut my door on the world, five things happened in this order:

A. Vlad handed me his pistol.

B. Rory promised to stand watch over me, waiting in case any more powerful emanations started coming my way.

C. Manhattan moved in with me that day. They'd be more likely to come for me outside the walls of the Choir's fortress and it was time we set our own traps.

D. Victor gave me a cane and showed me the spring that released its sheath from the blade.

E. Before he left, Victor looked at my shaking hands and asked if I was going to be okay. I was shaking and part of that was fear. Rage, however, ran far deeper and burned in the marrow of my bones. I looked Victor in the eyes and replied through gritted teeth, "I sing."

# 30

When Manhattan moved into my little apartment, all she had was a backpack. However, Victor sent gifts with her. The same truck that brought Manhattan also carried four young men. They brought five heavy, antique steamer trunks up the stairs.

The guys were all dressed in jeans and t-shirts and thick jackets. I could tell they were all part of the Choir Invisible. They were quiet and efficient. None of them flirted with Manhattan and they didn't hang around looking for a tip.

Those were clues, but it was their eyes that told me they were warriors. They all carried themselves with a subtle swagger, like cowboys with six guns strapped to their thighs. I didn't see any guns, but I assumed they were carrying. It was still unseasonably warm and I guessed those long, heavy jackets concealed weapons.

I'd seen their look before, in fighters' eyes at competitions. When I was in Mr. Chang's Hapkido school I met some fighters who were nervous. They tried to hide it by carrying their shoulders high, trying to look bigger than they really were. Others strode out, looking tough and confident in their abilities without a hint of self-consciousness. Either way, it was their energy I recognized.

Mr. Chang told me to beware of the humble fighters most. The ones who smiled and looked relaxed with nothing to prove had heads that were clearer. "Empty heads are more dangerous," he said.

By the time the movers left, Manhattan was already in the little kitchen setting up an espresso machine. "Nice little place, you've got here," she said. "Where's the rest of it?"

"You're looking at my entire empire, wall to wall."

"Even so, how can you afford this place, Iowa?"

I noticed she called me by my Choir name now, but I said nothing of it. "The short version is I beat a guy near to death, threatened to sue and collected a settlement."

"Ah. The old-fashioned American way to make money."

"Well, I — "

"No, that's good. Keep it to the short version."

"How long have you been in the Choir, Manhattan?"

"You may as well call me Manny, if you like. Fewer syllables."

"Okay. What a timesaver. Same question."

"I've served the Choir for five years."

"How did you find them?"

"They found me. I'd just turned fourteen the day my mother died. I was nineteen when Victor recruited me. This is a nice little vacation. I haven't lived outside the Keep since I joined up."

"Most of those boys…maybe most of the Choir…"

"Yeah, yeah. What?"

"They...our little army is not tested in battle are they?"

She frowned as she looked up from reading the instructions to the espresso machine. "Hey, dude, I just want to figure out how to make a latte, okay? Let's not make it too heavy between us on the first day."

"Manny? If we're going to live together and get through this, maybe you should climb down off my ass and answer my questions. I'll irritate you less in the long run if I'm up to speed."

What she gave me wasn't a smile, exactly, but she didn't roll her eyes or flip me off, either.

"You're right," she said, finally. "Here's the deal. Anyone in the Choir can see ghosts, but they haven't all fought yet. The demons don't come through in numbers. If they did, everybody would know about Armageddon. It would be here. Mr. Fuentes chooses well most of the time, though, so don't judge those guys just because they were on delivery duty. They're just...untested, as you put it. Just like you."

"Not like me," I said. "I castrated a monster this morning, remember?"

"Yeah. Thanks for the assist. Next time, go for the killing blow. Then it will count." She opened the old refrigerator. "You got cream?"

"Yeah. I keep it at the bodega down the street."

She looked around. "You need a few homey touches, farm girl." She pulled out her phone. "St. Charles? We've got some needs. Can you hook me up?" She didn't wait for a reply. "We're gonna need two beds, sheets and pillows. Send up something with a high thread count. I'm on vacation. Work on that now and I'll text you a list of groceries." She handed me the phone. "Make a list. You like soup? All I know how to make is vegetable soup. I presume all you eat is potatoes."

"That's Idaho," I said, "not Iowa."

I wasn't sure, but before she turned back to fiddling with her espresso machine, she might have let a half-smile slip out.

"Hey, girl. Christmas came early this year." She pointed to the steamer trunks. "Let's see what Mr. Fuentes sent us."

It seemed at first that all the first trunk contained was packing material. We had to dig through bubble wrap and styrofoam peanuts before we got to the trunk's contents. It was an orange lamp. It wasn't plugged in — there was no cord, in fact — but it was already glowing.

"I know what this is!" I said. "It's a salt lamp. It's supposed to kick out negative ions or positive ions. I forget which. It's supposed to be healthy."

"Nice try, rookie." Manhattan reached in and took one side of the lamp and motioned for me to help her.

I was surprised by its weight. "My god! Is it made of lead?" Between the two of us, we could hardly budge it.

"Lift with your legs or die," Manhattan said. When we lowered the lamp carefully to the floor, it sounded like we'd dropped a bowling ball.

As I stood, I caught movement out of the corner of my eye. Manny caught it, too and we were both ready for action. She pulled her gun from the holster in her waistband in one fluid motion.

I went into cat stance, ready to fight. Mr. Chang would have been proud. Manny laughed at me.

Before us in a recessed alcove, an old woman in a long dress walked back and forth. The apparition wore a hairnet. She was short and stout and waddled rather than walked. I had to squint to see her. She was almost transparent, but not quite.

Manhattan lowered her weapon. "Is that a smock or a frock? I always forget which is which, but I could rock a frock."

"What?"

"Relax, Iowa. Does that look like a demon to you?"

"I've only seen one. I don't know what they all look like."

"It's just a fade. We call them echoes, too. Look at her. She's barely there at all."

"Is she like Rory?"

"No. Rory's a ghost. That's an echo."

"An echo of what?"

"An old lady who used to live here. She's so faint, she's more like an after-image, isn't she? Relax."

"The old woman who lived here died just before I moved in."

"Nah. When they are that faded, that's not a ghost. That's an echo of someone who lived here long before we were born. Look at the way she's dressed. That's an echo of *old* New York. I've never seen anyone wear a hairnet outside of a fast food joint, have you?"

I studied the woman as she walked back and forth. She repeated the same movements, like a loop of damaged black and white film.

"That," Manhattan said, "is anguish. See how she touches her face over and over? When humans comfort themselves, they touch their faces a lot. Just like that."

"Where'd you pick that up?"

"Grief counseling. Dead mother at fourteen,

remember? Dad insisted I was crazy from grief when I said I could see her in the driver's seat every time the Volvo was parked in the garage. Every time the garage door came down, there was Mom, killing herself again."

"I'm sorry, Manny."

She shrugged. "She doesn't do it anymore. After I joined the choir, I went back with a blessed blade and WIC allowed her to move on to the next level."

"WIC?"

"Whoever's in Charge."

"You mean God?"

"We don't use that term. It's...imprecise and causes arguments. The Choir incorporates many religious faiths in the struggle against evil. There's more harmony among the Choir sections if we're as non-denominational as possible."

"Um...okay. Let's leave that for now. I'm more concerned the heavy salt lamp that looks like it came from Pier 1 Imports is showing me a grief-stricken woman in my apartment."

Manny smiled. "The echo shows the strength of her emotional pain when she was mortal. The emotional pain was so great, she left an energy imprint in that spot."

"Does it have to be anguish that leaves a mark?"

"No. Rory tells me that birthing rooms in hospitals are filled with imprints of joy...mostly."

Manhattan began putting the packing material back in the lamp's steamer trunk.

"What exactly is the difference between an echo and a ghost?" I asked.

"Ghosts, you've seen. They're us, but dead and not gone. Echoes are...I dunno. Echoes. There's no *sentience* to an echo."

I stared at her and quirked an eyebrow.

She tried again. "Victor says that we all leave skin cells behind. You plant a couch in front of a TV for twenty years, there's a lot of you in that couch, right? Same with energy. We leave behind energy signatures, like an echo in a cavern, except this one goes on for a long time before it fades out. That chick went on to heaven or wherever a long time ago. The lamp of Tighloon is an amplifier. Her energy is so weak that, without the lamp, not even Rory would have seen her there. Echoes are everywhere."

"Rory didn't see the demon last night," I said.

"The thing was cloaked. Some enchantment Ra has been experimenting with. It's not perfect, but it spells trouble. I want the Darkness Visible to stay visible. Still, it wouldn't have made a difference if Rory had seen exactly what was coming. No matter where I go, I expect the humans to be packing Howitzers and I anticipate a demon horde pouring out of every bathroom, armed to the fangs. Paranoia works. I don't care who it is. If a station wagon full of nuns stops and asks for directions, suspect suicide vests and Uzis first."

(That's Lesson 61, kids!)

"Aside from kind of freaking me out, what does the lamp do?"

"Early warning system. If the light begins to get brighter, you've got demons coming to dinner. Rory's going to stick close to you. If he's needed elsewhere, the lamp is a failsafe. You've got nothing to worry about. You're here, so what could possibly go wrong except I might get beheaded like Bronx?"

We watched the echo of a woman long dead walk back

195

and forth. After a while, Manhattan dug a canteen out of her gear and splashed what looked like water on the floor where the woman walked.

In a blink, the echo was gone and the lamp of Tighloon faded to a low ebb, no brighter than a dim nightlight.

"What is that stuff?" I asked.

Manhattan poured some liquid out of the canteen into the palm of her hand and splashed her face and neck with it.

"*Agh! Holy water!* It burns! It *burns!*" she screamed, then collapsed into giggles.

# 31

When I stopped laughing, I asked Manhattan a serious question. "The lamp didn't go out. Shouldn't the lamp go out? *Why didn't the lamp go out?*"

"Dude! Evil's never *that* far away. I've never seen a lamp of Tighloon go out completely. It's not just for demons. It detects really bad humans, too."

"Well. There's one to grow on. The WIC thing...we don't have to talk God — "

"I'd rather not," she said.

"Okay, but where do you think we go when we die? Do you believe in heaven? Or hell, or, at least...I dunno... having a rest?"

Manhattan shrugged. "I believe in next. Dead or alive, there's a next, I think. I don't know what it will be. Victor says we travel the multiverse in all its infinite possibilities. You might become a silkworm on a planet run by reptiles who only allow *Ironman* versus *Godzilla* movies."

"If it's run by reptiles, Godzilla would always win."

"Well," Manhattan fluttered her hands, "*random!*"

"Do you think Victor knows what he's talking about?"

"I think sometimes Victor tells people what they want to hear. That's not as bad as it sounds. I think he believes what he says, too. But he also doesn't talk much about what's next when Vlad is around. The big man can't help himself, poking holes."

"Does that mean Vlad knows?"

"No. Vlad is better at seeing what's false. That doesn't mean he knows what's true."

"Have you asked Vlad what he thinks?"

"I don't like talking about next," Manhattan said. "We'll all find out soon enough. Got another question? A better one?"

"Okay. The demons really want to eat us?"

"They aren't lacto-ovo vegetarian."

"Go on."

Manhattan gazed at me steadily. "They like chocolate, pizza and human entrails. I don't know if they are invading our dimension just for our guts or the promise of pizza delivered to your door in less than thirty minutes."

I giggled.

Manny did not. I really didn't know if she was messing with me about the chocolate and pizza. I still wasn't sure when she promised she wasn't lying.

"Okay," I said. "On a related note, let's see if Victor sent us a ton of weapons."

The second trunk did indeed hold guns. There were a couple of assault rifles and several smaller weapons that could be concealed.

"You know your way around a pistol?" Manny asked.

"I'm from Iowa."

"Is that a yes?"

"It is." Mama owned a shotgun, a deer rifle and she

had three pistols. She practiced with them once a month at the range. "In case that man ever thinks about coming back," Mama said.

I suspected now that Mama was target shooting in preparation for an invasion of a demon horde. I hadn't called Mama and I hadn't answered her texts. I wasn't ready to confront her with what I knew yet.

"The important thing isn't so much the weapons," Manhattan said. "It's the ammo. Every bullet and cartridge has been blessed three times by three senior priests from three different religions. Three is a power number. I prefer when celibate monks bless my ammo. Makes me feel like I've given them one thing to do that's worthwhile."

"Victor said bullets don't work as well as blades."

"Not the bullets you buy from Walmart. Swords are much better. Blessed blades are like getting cut with a sword, plus an acid bath for the enemy. Still, use enough of the right kind of bullets and you can bring anything down. It still usually takes a lot of holy rounds with the big demons."

"Your bullets worked on Brooks fine."

"Yep. Blessed by celibate priests or not, humans are more vulnerable to high speed iron supplements."

"You okay with that?" I asked. She'd only helped kill a man and a demon that morning, but Manhattan looked plenty steady to me. When I thought about it, my hands still shook and butterflies with iron wings tried to escape my stomach.

"Brooks wasn't the first human I've shot, Iowa. He won't be the last. Victor talks a good game to the troops about holding back Armageddon, but the invasion is inevitable. Then the world will see what's real. When the shit hits the ceiling fan, you find out who your real friends are. Plenty of humans will collaborate with the enemy. At first they'll do it out of fear or because they think they'll be spared. In the end, though, we're all bowel and pancreas pizza unless we kill Ra's forces first."

I watched her for a moment. I didn't doubt her conviction, but what was missing was any mention of Bronx. Like Victor said, people often fail to notice what isn't there. "Was Bronx your boyfriend?" I asked.

"No," she said. "I prefer girls, but Bronx was a friend. Victor says, '*Quem Di diligent, adolescens moritur.*'"

"*What?*"

"It's Latin, from a Billy Joel song or something, I think. *Only the good die young.*"

She moved to the window to watch Church Avenue. "Bronx's real name was Josh. He saved my life twice. The first time was when he found me, suicidal in a cemetery next to my mother's grave. I was staring at all the damned outside the fence, waiting to be let in so they could lie down. They were looking for peace and salvation and so was I. When Josh found me…I had a knife at my wrist.

"I told him to go away, but he just stood there, watching and waiting. He told me how to do it right. For the most blood, he told me not to cut across the wrists. 'Cut down the arm if you're serious,' he said. Then he said if I did it, I might have to join the ghost parade outside the fence and wait a long time to really die.

"I asked him why," Manhattan said, "and he said he didn't think we get to go to bed and pull the covers over our heads. We don't get to retreat from life. We have to go get it. I looked at all the dead along the fence who used to be people. Then I buried the knife in the dirt at my mother's grave. I started bawling my eyes out again and I asked him what I should do. He told me he sang and I should, too. Then he brought me to Victor Fuentes. That's how I joined the Choir Invisible."

I didn't know what to say so I said nothing. That's one of my talents.

After a while, Manhattan continued. "Josh said to call him Bronx. He was one of my first trainers," — she hefted her sword parasol — "so I could be a singer, too."

"What was the second time he saved your life?"

"Last night," she said, "when I said I'd take point and he said no."

"I'm so sorry."

"Me, too."

"Do you want to talk about it, Manny?"

"No."

The next trunk held two katanas and two short swords. "We've already got swords," I said.

"These aren't for concealment. These are for when the big battle comes to town." Manhattan smiled so wide, I wondered if she was looking forward to the bloodbath to come. It took me a moment to figure out that's exactly what she wanted. Manny wanted vengeance.

The swords were beautiful works of art. I had seen replicas, but the authentic swords shone with lethality. I ached to hold one. "Ever since I saw Uma Thurman kick ass in *Kill Bill*, I wanted swords and a yellow and black track suit. Mr. Chang trained me in kendo."

"Kevin Chang?" she said.

"What?"

"Kevin Chang," she repeated. "He's also my master in

201

bujutsu. He hates Iowa, but your Mama and Victor and Peter all knew, the children of the Armageddon Savants must be trained." When she caught the look on my face, she laughed.

"Mr. Chang told me he was an accountant," I said.

"He is," she said. "People can be more than one thing."

I sat on the floor by the lamp of Tighloon and thought how strange it was that I was sitting by a magical lamp. But that didn't feel all that strange, anymore. The lamp was just a small miracle now.

Lesson 62: You can get used to a lot of things pretty fast, but never betrayal. You never get over feeling like a fool. You never bounce back from discovering your whole life is a lie and the people you trust most are liars.

Manhattan didn't open the last trunk and when I moved to do so, she shook her head. "That one is full of explosives," she said. "Gimme your phone. I'll put the detonator code on speed dial for you. Don't press the contact for Heaven unless you need to. You'll know when you need to."

"How will I know, Manny?" I asked.

"Oh, Iowa," she said. "A demon will be chewing through your sweetbreads."

I was a long time falling asleep that night. I was almost dreaming when I remembered the beautiful girl with the mocha skin in the next bed had said she preferred girls.

Demons, predators, espresso-loving lesbians! Oh, my! When you look at the big picture, minus all the magic drama, New York was shaping up to be pretty much how I expected.

# 32

The next day it rained and I stayed inside with Manny. In the morning I tried to impress her with the number of pushups I could do without stopping. That urge faded fast when she pointedly ignored me so she could set up a modem for wifi. Although I'd been hiking all over New York City, my upper body strength had waned over the summer.

I ended up sweating through planks and crunches and was tapped out faster than I expected. Mr. Chang was always challenging me to go "just one more minute." At the end of sixty seconds, he would say again, "just one more minute. You can do *anything* for a minute!"

The "one more minute" didn't stop coming, of course. Not until I collapsed.

The grueling workouts made more sense now. He'd told each of his students that what we learned from him might one day save our lives. Though he was talking to everyone, his comments were aimed at me. And all along, Mama and Mr. Chang had made me think studying Hapkido and Kendo so diligently was my idea.

By ten o'clock I was tired and showered and in need of a distraction, anything to stop thinking about demons. The quintessential thing to do in New York on a rainy day when you're shut in and waiting to be attacked by otherworldly monsters with long fangs? Read a book. Reading any book in my apartment in New York (complete with a fresh cappuccino) seemed more weighty and pretentious than reading on my bed in Medicament, Iowa. I downloaded *The Fault in Our Stars* by John Green to my phone. I liked the funny observations and witty dialogue very much, but I couldn't face teenagers dealing with cancer that day.

By noon, I was hungry and suffering a terrible case of cabin fever. Manny sat on the floor in full lotus position and didn't look up from tapping on her laptop. Her big glasses had slid to the end of her nose.

I finally asked her what she was doing. "Mm. I was looking at the inventory at the Keep and e-mailing St. Charles that we should stock up on baby formula and diapers. When Armageddon hits, we could loot that stuff later, but I think we should pay for it now. We don't want to have to go out on runs for Baby Mum Mums crackers at the last minute. Not with babies screaming in our ears. Baby cries are the worst."

"What else?"

"I was plotting fallback positions. If the Keep is breached and there are survivors, I was thinking we should go to a Costco. Victor suggested a well-known place for a rendezvous point, like the Guggenheim or the Cathedral of St. John the Divine. The Cathedral isn't bad. It's the largest church in the city, over on Amsterdam. Demons do not like churches and might be put off searching and destroying us there. For a while."

"Victor told me. Something about vibes in the bricks."

"Good and Evil," she said. "One of the few constants across the realms. But it's not like demons are vampires. They don't like churches, but they will go in if they have to. Makes them irritable. Maybe gives them a rash, I don't know. We don't know enough about the enemy. That's one of the reasons we're so screwed."

She looked up a moment and must have read the horrified expression on my face. "*Art of War*: know your enemy or he will mess you up until you are peeing out your ears and begging for death."

I suspect Manny was paraphrasing *The Art of War* somewhat, but that's Lesson 63.

Then I remembered something. "Victor told me, 'Death must be met,' is one of the few constants across dimensions."

"Victor has a bunch of canned speeches." Manhattan pushed her glasses up and went back to her screen. "He's been at this war a long time. Anyway, I'm recommending we switch the retreat position to the nearest Costco. In fact, we should have a plan for multiple Costcos for survivors to retreat to. Always plan the exit strategy first." (And that, you guessed it, is Lesson 64.)

"What about the demons?" I asked. "Won't they like Costco? They can probably get pizza dough in bulk there."

Manny shook her head and smiled. "They'll like them less if we send out teams of monks, priests and ministers to go stand at the four walls of each Costco to bless the buildings. Any place can be a sacred space, as long as the faith is strong enough."

"Then why not bless all of New York City, or the planet?"

"We can try, but that's a lot of buildings and it's just a minor deterrent. It slows down the Darkness Visible. I told you. They aren't vampires."

"Are there such things as vampires?"

"Yup. Energy vampires." She looked at me pointedly. "They distract people from their work."

I was about to apologize for bothering her, but as I walked behind her, I caught a glimpse of what was on her screen. Manhattan was looking at pictures of cute little baby pigs on Pinterest. "Really?" I said.

She frowned. "I'm taking a break!"

"*Really?*"

Then she gave me a wide smile, showing off her perfect, even teeth. "I'm taking a break from Facebook, Twitter and porn."

"Oh..." — deep breath — "my *WIC!*" I said. "And I've just been sitting here contemplating what it will feel like to die screaming as a demon makes a happy meal out of me."

"Work on your abs," she suggested.

"Abs of steel won't stop fangs."

Manny put the laptop down and rose from the floor without using her hands. (Try it from full lotus. It's not easy.) "Okay," she said. "It's past time we really got you up to speed. Let's go. Everybody needs initiation. It's your day. Time to strut your stuff, Iowa."

I looked outside. A cold downpour soaked the streets. "It's raining really hard."

"Do you think the Marines stop training outside whenever it sprinkles?"

"No, but — "

"Look in the third trunk," she said. "There are a couple of big umbrellas in there."

"What does my initiation consist of? I don't like the sound of that."

"It's fun," Manhattan said.

"Really?"

"Well, not for you, but the rest of us will have a great time."

"I haven't decided yet whether I like you," I said.

Manhattan smirked. "Put that off until after the initiation ceremony. If you judge me by what happens today, we'll never be friends."

"I think I might hate you now," I said.

Manny smiled wider.

# 33

A cab returned us to the Keep and Manny took me to her room to change. "You'll need some armor. You're about my size, a little shorter," she said. "Try this."

She held out a tunic.

"What is that?"

"It's old," she said. "It's called scale armor. See? The scales overlap and it's hard leather underneath."

I slipped the tunic over my head. It was lighter than I expected. "What is this made of?"

"Pangolin."

"That sounds pretty. What's that?"

"It's a kind of anteater."

"*What?*"

Manny pulled me by the tunic and shoved a football helmet into my hands. "Stop being a baby."

"I'm wearing an *anteater!*"

"C'mon. It's from long before pangolins were endangered...I think."

A few minutes later, we stood in the central courtyard. Despite the rain, sword practice continued. When I'd looked at the courtyard with Victor, we were far up. I hadn't noticed from on high, but many of the pads that served as the training ground for the Choir Invisible were not merely flat concrete. Some pads were elevated at one end. Some were constructed of soft padding. Others were made of sand or cobblestone.

As Manny strode to the edge of the concentric circles of pads, Rory appeared beside me. "Hello, m'lady."

"Hi, Rory." When I glanced sideways, the dead man's eyes had gone dark instead of their blazing orange. Black pits where eyes should be are disconcerting, but I tried to show no sign I was freaking out. I didn't want to accidentally channel anyone again. The visions weren't worth the nausea. I was fidgety, so I asked Rory a question, just to make small talk. "Do ghosts watch TV?"

"For many of us, that's all we do. Eternity can be so incredibly boring. You have to be careful to keep yourself occupied and productive. That's why I'm here. At least, that's why I'm partially here."

"Where else are you?"

"I'm monitoring a pedophile's whereabouts in the Village. I'm also in Scotland at the moment."

"What awful thing draws you to Scotland?"

"Nothing awful at the moment. I just love Edinburgh. It's lovely. I love the architecture."

"Oh."

"Even the dead must have a life," Rory said.

Manny startled me by singing. It was one high note, but it was clear and beautiful. Every member of the Choir Invisible stopped in the midst of training to look. Then they all answered with a note of their own. I can't say it was beautiful exactly. It was more startling than beautiful.

209

Then the voices rose and rose and harmonized. Their peculiar music became kind of lovely and fierce at the same time. I'd have enjoyed it more if I wasn't about to… well, I didn't know what I was about to do.

Mr. Chang's ritual at the beginning of each of his classes was to say that, one day, each of us would be tested. I thought he was just speaking of grading for belts. I knew better now.

"They won't expect anything much from you, child," Rory said. "Give 'em a surprise or two, eh? That wouldn't be boring."

Once Manhattan saw that every eye was on her, she raised a hand and closed her fist. The Choir stopped. She announced, "By now, you all know we have lost Bronx!"

Everyone bowed their head and, as one, chanted, "Bronx has fallen. Bronx is lost. As we go, so goes the world. We are the Choir. That is the cost."

"We have a new member of the Choir Invisible! She helped avenge the demon that took Bronx from us."

"That wasn't vengeance," I whispered to Rory. "That was desperation and self-defense."

"*Sh.* Keep your end up, girl," Rory replied. "Do try to look dangerous and capable so they'll *value* you."

"Today," Manny continued, "she joins us in struggle and service." The sky was black and the rain came harder as Manny turned and called to me so everyone could hear. "Candidate! Name your cause so we will know your effect!"

I blanked out. All I could think of was my dead boyfriend holding a Superman comic. "T-truth, j-justice and the American Way?"

Fortunately, no one heard me above the hammering

rain. Rory might have heard me, but he didn't get it. The dead man leaned close and I could feel how cold he was. "Your *name*," he said. "What place do you champion?"

I wanted to say *everywhere*. Instead, I called out, "Iowa!"

Every member of the Choir Invisible chanted three times, "Iowa is risen. Iowa is found. As Iowa goes, so goes the world. We are the Choir. We stand our ground."

Manhattan nodded. "Step forward, candidate."

I stared and Rory chuckled. "Go on, then. Take your medicine. I'll walk with you and talk you through it."

I walked toward Manhattan through mud. Or maybe that was just my legs not wanting to work.

"Three is the power number!" Manny called. "Do I have three defenders?"

Everyone in the courtyard raised their swords. Manny pointed to three singers and the rest retreated to the far side of the field of training pads.

Manny motioned for me to come closer and dipped into a big trunk at her side that looked much like the steamer trunks we'd left in my apartment.

I thought of my tiny, warm apartment with an espresso machine on the counter and chicken noodle soup on the stove. *The Fault in Our Stars* was still spread upside down on my bed. I was pissed at Manny, and myself, too. I should have stayed home.

Manny pulled out a couple of gloves with long, hard gauntlets to protect my forearms. "Don't worry," she said. "It's no big deal. Every military organization has a ritual. This is ours."

"What do I do? They aren't going to ask me to dance, will they? I look weird when I dance." But I already knew what was going to happen. I was going to get my ass

211

kicked.

"Relax. I'm pretty sure you can take two of the three singers I picked."

"*Two* of three?"

"It's a game," Manhattan said.

"Oh, it's no game," Rory said. "Monopoly is a game. I've never seen anyone lose teeth or break a wrist in a parlor game of any sort."

"*Teeth?*"

"Teeth can be replaced. Did I mention you should relax?" Manny asked. "I probably did."

I looked to the three swordsmen with whom I was about to do battle. All three wore helmets which obscured their faces and each helmet's mask was a face. They were not human faces. Their protective masks were all scary demon faces.

The first opponent looked lean and quick. The second was big and brawny. The last, near the center of the clutch of circles, slid one hand across his neck in the universal sign for "You're buzzard meat."

I was out of sorts so, whether or not there actually are buzzards throughout the universe, you get the idea. I could hear the pulse in my ears already. "I'm in the wrong place," I said.

Manhattan grabbed my head with both hands and forced me to look in her eyes and yelled for everyone's benefit, maybe even my own, "Iowa, Castrator of Demons, live up to your name!"

"Ah," I said. "Okay."

Manny whispered, "You don't have to win. You just have to fight. This is for real."

"This is happening," I said.

Manny looked fierce. "If you can't face us, you can't face the Darkness Visible. If you can't sing with the Choir, you're right. You are in the wrong place. What's it going to be? Are you a girl named Tammy or are you a soprano named Iowa?"

I turned to face the trio of defenders, mostly because I was pissed at Manny. She handed me a wooden sword painted black. It was a *bokken*. I was more used to using a *shinai* sword, a loose bundle of bamboo tied together in such a way that, even if swung hard, the weapon didn't really hurt. Bokkens are solid wood. They hurt.

Lesson 65: Whether you're joining the PTA, the Choir Invisible or a knitting club, inquire ahead of time about initiation rites. Know what to expect. I wish I had. However, not knowing what I was getting into was probably part of the test.

Manhattan tied a thick cloth belt around my middle and cinched it tight over my anteater armor. I felt something heavy at my waist. When I looked down, I expected to find a dagger. Instead, I found a taser. "For if you get up close," Manny said.

"*If?*"

"Sometimes this ends really quickly. Good luck."

"If you donned your helmet now, m'lady," Rory said, "that would not be amiss."

I fumbled with my helmet. I hadn't paid attention to it before. It was a New York Giants football helmet with a visor to protect my eyes. I noticed it would not protect my teeth.

"The goal," Rory explained, "is to get to the center circle."

"What if I just run for it?"

"Then all three will come at you at once."

"So I have to take them on one at a time?"

"That would be my advice, yes," Rory said.

"What if I don't get past the first one?"

"Once you're down, I am almost sure they will stop fairly soon." His chuckle sounded like a stone bumping down a long pipe into a well. "Once you step on the pad, you must stay on the pad or you lose. You don't have to win. You just have to try. No one expects you to win."

*No one expects you to win.* That really pissed me off. I took the sword handle in both hands. "I don't have to *win?* That's not how I play. Not since Shibboleth."

"That's fine," Rory said, "I would advise against gritting your teeth like that. It makes your lovely smile more…vulnerable. Gritted teeth are more easily chipped."

With a dead man by my side, I took on the my first opponent in the Choir Invisible.

Lesson 66: If possible and for a greater chance of success, advance on your enemy with lots of live, well-armed men and women by your side.

I went into the first test alone, of course. In the end, when we face our greatest tests, we're always alone.

# 34

**T**he first pad was not just a solid black pad. As I came closer, I realized it was a trampoline.

I assumed the first swordsman would have the wisdom to feel me out a bit to test my tactics before launching into an all-out attack. Instead, the tall and stringy fighter jumped and came at me off a high bounce. He screamed a war cry.

Lesson 67: Aggression and striking first often wins, but rushing at an unknown enemy is foolish. The way he attacked, I was sure he not only wanted to win, but he was showing off, as well. Mama would have called his problem, "testosterone poisoning."

Mr. Chang taught me what he called the Economy of the Sword. You keep your sword out in front, the pointy end toward the opponent at a forty-five degree angle. You do not reach to block an attack because a miss is as good as a mile. If you reach to block, you may lose your center of balance and you can be pushed or pulled into a vulnerable position.

There's another law of physics that applies the next

time somebody comes at you off a trampoline with a sword. When the attacker jumps off a trampoline at an opponent, he can't change course in mid-air. I dodged left, ducked and swept my bokken into his shins.

*Crack!*

His scream turned from a war cry into a simple cry. My attacker's momentum carried him off the pad and he landed on his face hard. He rolled around in the mud rubbing his shins. When he pulled up his helmet's visor, I saw I'd been fighting a boy. He might have been fifteen. He squinted up at me and cursed at me in his pain.

Lesson 68: Research studies have shown that cursing lessens pain. Indulge in cursing if you're in a lot of pain. If you're the one causing the pain instead of suffering it, victory helps you get past any hurt feelings. Smile. Bow. It annoys the shit out of the loser.

The Choir chanted, "Delaware has fallen. Delaware has failed. Delaware is lost."

*Ouch.* No wonder the kid felt he had something to prove. I bounced across the trampoline pad. As I made my way from pad to pad, I had to admit, the Choir's training area was impressive. One pad was made entirely of steps in concentric circles. Another was a shallow pit which would drive the combatants together. Then came a pad that was a forest of thin steel poles.

The bulky and brawny fighter awaited me on a concrete pad that was raised in the middle. As I got closer, the swordsman raised his visor. It wasn't a he. I faced a smiling, freckle faced black woman.

"Hi," I said.

"I'm Wilmington," she said. "Wilmington, Vermont. I don't fall." She brought her visor down and in one smooth motion, swung her sword at mine, trying to knock it from my hands. I felt the wind of the wooden blade's arc as I circled left.

Wilmington was a canny fighter. She stayed to the center of the pad. Keeping the high ground to place me at a disadvantage. She attacked with strong, overhead strikes that drove me back. In refusing to give up her advantage, she would not stray from the center of the pad to press her attack.

*Clack! Clack! Clack!*

I blocked her *bokken* and waited and watched as she shuffled forward and back, always returning to the center. She was strong and confident, but she only thought with her weapon and she repeated the same attack too often.

As she came at me again, I broke the rhythm that she had fallen into with an attack of my own. She blocked me and I tried to lure her out. As soon as she realized she had strayed from the pad's high center, she began to retreat. Her momentum was already going backward and I switched to a ferocious attack that kept her in retreat.

When her rear heel hit the edge of the pad she stopped just in time and threw herself forward. I switched tactics, stepped to her right and smashed my right gauntlet into her visor with the back of my gloved fist.

Wilmington's head rocked back but, true to her word, she did not fall. Off balance, she raised her sword high to bring it down on my head. I dropped to the ground and swept my right heel under her feet. She pinwheeled backward off the pad to land on her back.

The Choir chanted, "Wilmington has fallen. Wilmington has failed. Wilmington is lost." But our audience applauded, too.

"Iowa! Iowa! Iowa!"

When I looked up, I saw a friendly face I recognized. It was St. Charles, clapping and cheering for me from his high window up in the library.

I gave him a thumbs up and bowed to Wilmington. She raised her visor and gave me a smile. "Good one."

I made my way around the pad, taking my time so I could catch my breath.

The second to last pad was flat, but as small as a large elevator. My opponent was dressed head to toe in ornate red armor that looked like it was made of shiny enamel. His throat was exposed, but that was all.

"I am *so* screwed," I told him.

He nodded and took up his sword. Unlike the others, he waited for me to attack. Stepping on the small pad, the tips of our swords already touched.

I tried circling his sword with mine to close the distance. He batted my bokken away with a strong stroke and I nearly dropped it.

Lesson 69: This, I learned from Mr. Chang. It's about fire and water. He may or may not have picked it up from reading about Bruce Lee. He claimed he couldn't remember.

In a water attack, you flow around your opponent's advances and strike at him without engaging his defenses. With the fire strategy, you do not attack his head or torso, but instead, you burn whatever he uses to reach you. If he kicks, you don't simply block. You try to shatter his ankle with your weapon or your elbows. If he comes at you with a sword, smash and cut at his hands.

I tried the fire approach. My opponent used the water attack to put me out.

Lesson 70: when your opponent knows your moves, you have to come up with new moves very quickly.

I was driven to my knees. I wasn't holding my sword anymore and my left arm was throbbing at the bicep. The flat of his sword came down hard on my shoulder and I cried out as I fell to my hands and knees. I was in perfect beheading position, though I hoped that wasn't the end goal of my initiation into the Choir.

I tried to roll under his feet to bowl him over. He laughed as he leapt over me. When I sat up, my opponent was holding his bokken and mine, too, one in each hand.

He took a step closer and put the tip of his sword under my exposed throat to tilt my head back.

"This is the time when I'm supposed to give up, right?"

My silent opponent gave me a slow, sage nod.

Rory appeared at the edge of the pad. "Well done, girl. No shame in this performance."

The man in the enamel armor nodded to the dead man and lowered the tip of my bokken an inch from my throat. I wrapped my ankles around my attacker's forward foot, grabbed the wooden blade with one hand and pulled my opponent into the crackle of my taser.

Just before the electric blue arc could touch his throat, he swept my weapon away. It landed in a mud puddle, far from my reach.

My attacker pulled me to my feet, laughing at me again. The more he laughed, the more my rage built. He was clearly the superior fighter.

He backed away and stuck the tips of my bokken and his in the mud at the edge of the pad. He was still chuckling when he came back to face me empty-handed.

I grabbed his helmet with both hands and tried to twist,

but before I could throw him, he threw me to the pad. Fast and sure, he locked down on my wrist so hard that, even through my gauntlet, I thought he might break bone.

"Did I mention you've already done well?" Rory asked, louder this time. "It's time to surrender, girl! Do not be embarrassed."

"I'm not embarrassed," I whispered. "I'm *fighting*."

My opponent finally spoke. "But do you know when to give up?"

I knew that voice. He eased his grip as he lifted his visor and I stared up into Mr. Chang's face. He smiled and pulled me up. I stood before my teacher.

I spit in his eye and slammed my New York Giants football helmet into his nose. He reeled back and stood holding his nose as blood poured out. But Mr. Chang was still on the pad. And still smiling.

I ripped off my helmet. I gave Mr. Chang a big, cheery smile and stepped toward him, offering my hand to shake. "Mr. Chang! It's so good to see you! I'm so glad you're in New York! Do you miss Iowa at all yet?" Before he could answer, I whispered, "you will."

He dropped his guard for a split second. That's all it takes. I swung my helmet at his head as hard as I could and it clanged off the side of his fancy helmet. I knocked Mr. Chang off the edge of the pad.

He didn't go down so I didn't accept that I'd won until my teacher bowed. "You had a good teacher," he said.

"Yes," I said. "Though I've learned a little more ruthlessness since. You shouldn't have let Mama send me to that mental hospital, sir."

Mr. Chang bowed again, deeper this time. As apologies go, it wasn't an iTunes gift certificate and a spa day, but it would have to do.

The Choir stood in stunned silence and incomprehension as they watched our exchange, though one member was clapping madly and laughing. St. Charles waved to me from his perch in the high library window.

I took up my black *bokken* and strode to the smallest pad at the center of all the circles. I raised my sword high. "My name is Iowa, Castrator of Demons, and I'm too dumb to know when to quit!"

St. Charles hooted his approval and the singers raised their swords, laughing and cheering. This time, the Choir's chant was a roar as they repeated three times, "Iowa has risen. Iowa has won. Iowa is among the Choir Invisible. Her battle is done!"

Lesson 71: Sometimes (okay, *rarely*) superior force can be defeated by being sneaky and too stupid to quit. I recommend being the superior force. Overwhelm the enemy with your genius and strength. If you don't have those advantages, that doesn't necessarily mean the fight is over.

The last time I had spoken to Mr. Chang, I was still in Medicament. After meeting the evil Dr. Moorely, losing meant much more to me than simply admitting I'd failed. Losing meant submission. Submitting meant nullification. Losing meant I counted for nothing. I wasn't the same person as I'd been in Medicament. I couldn't be. People change, either under very good circumstances or facing horror.

Standing in the center of the Keep's courtyard, holding my sword high, I felt I'd endured tragedy, but triumph and exhilaration rushed through my blood, too.

For a brief moment, Brad was not with me. I had no grief to carry. In victory, just for a moment, it was okay to forget him. I didn't have to mourn not being part of a pair, anymore. I didn't have to face the world alone, either. I had an army of outcasts and freaks just like me on my side. We could see ghosts and we fought evil demons and we'd do it all together. And, I was sure, we would win.

The Choir rushed to the center of the courtyard, shouting and laughing, to welcome me to their number. Theirs was a music only new comrades united against a common enemy could make.

But the enemy composes symphonies of anguish and destruction. War cries that were not our own filled the air, thicker than the streaming rain, as the library exploded.

# 35

St. Charles was blown out of the library window. He fell into the courtyard, lifeless and aflame.

It wasn't exactly an explosion. The demons tore a rift between dimensions. A dozen came pouring out of the crack they'd made in the membrane between their hellscape and our world. I don't know magic, but whatever they did worked.

I saw St. Charles hit the ground, loose jointed and head first. I cringed as his neck snapped and his head bent over to one shoulder at a crazy angle. The sight made my stomach flip.

I wondered what his real name had been. After we die, whatever names we took on and whatever we pretend to be, goes away. We are reduced. It was a strange battlefield reaction, but I stood frozen a moment as the boy burned.

What got me moving was the sight of the demons. The one in Carl Brooks' basement had been as black and shiny as onyx. The warriors that dropped to the courtyard grounds had skin as red as cartoon devils. They looked like they should carry pitchforks. Instead, swords hung sheathed at their waists and they held long spears with three cruel points.

*Tridents,* I thought. *Like Neptune.*

Flames lit the hole that had been the library window. Two demons, their skin shining a radiant blue, appeared together. The pair roared, their words echoing off the Keep's walls in unison. *"We are Gog and Magog!"*

Lesson 72: Never underestimate your enemy. Most demons are physically strong and they have the uncanny ability to make your heart race. They smell fear just as dogs do and, unlike ghosts, you can never get used to them. They smell like cabbage and dirty feet (and most do, in fact, go barefoot.)

They are of varied races, but you'll rarely see a short one or, thank god, a child demon. Some have horns that look like antlers and others have no horns at all. Perhaps because of where they come from, they don't mind the heat and hate the cold.

Demons can laugh, and often do, but they rarely laugh at anything we'd find funny. Usually it's derisive laughter at the suffering and humiliation of others. They look upon humans as cattle to be slaughtered. If one of them took a liking to a human, the friendship would be fleeting since they bore easily. Though curious about us, we are inferior animals in their eyes.

Their curiosity about our world seems to be limited to our food and music. We know they enjoy our alcoholic beverages, architecture and war machines. Mostly, they're all about the conquering.

When the two blue demons appeared, there was no follow up to, "We are Gog and Magog!"

Lesson 73: Demons are not big on speeches.

The first demons to jump into the courtyard killed several members of the Choir where they lay dazed from the explosion. The red monsters stuck their tridents through our members' backs and twisted as they pulled the barbed blades away. Their weapons dripped with blood and gore.

I saw several of the largest of our men rush at the demons. They only had wooden practice swords, but they did not use their weapons as swords. They held the bokkens at each end and pushed up under the monsters' throats, shoving them back into the courtyard's stone walls.

The blessings and prayers of generations of ministers, priests, congregations, nuns and monks still held power. Though the demons towered above the humans, the men managed to pin two against the stone wall. One screamed in anguish and threw off his attackers. The other burst into flames and soon fell by the charred remains of St. Charles.

The demon who had swept away two grown men in rage was weakened by his contact with the wall. His back smoked and he howled with pain.

Though battered, three men of the Choir came at the weakened one before more invaders could come to their comrade's rescue.

One man slipped behind the monster and went to his hands and knees as two more men threw themselves at the demon's torso. The evil thing fell backward, tripping over the man on his hands and knees. When the demon's head hit the Keep's blessed wall, it split open like a watermelon.

As soon as more demons hit the ground, they killed the men who had taken their two soldiers. They ripped and tore with their tridents. Demons are sadists. They take their time and pleasure in the slaughter.

The Choir lost good and brave soldiers in the first minute of the battle for the Keep. However, the red demons' cruelty did yield one advantage to our side: time. The Choir fled.

Rory appeared at my side again. "Despite what you said about not knowing when to quit, this is an excellent time to run. Call it a strategic retreat."

"Huh?"

"Go!" Rory pointed to my left, through the west arch of the central courtyard toward the ruins of the church at the base of the bailey.

The Choir swarmed past me, running from the demon invasion. There were only a dozen of the enemy, but they were formidable. Pitting our wooden practice swords against their tridents was not a winning strategy for us.

But those in the east courtyard did not practice with swords. The Choir's archers practiced there. There weren't many Choir members armed with bows and arrows, but it was soon apparent their steel tips and razor edges were blessed. The archers rushed forward to support our sword section's retreat to the barracks.

As the red invaders ran through the circle of training pads, arrows tore through them. Demons bellowed in anguish. Many of the arrows missed. It is not easy to hit a running demon at forty yards, but the flight of arrows loosed on the monsters brought down three.

That left seven red demons by my count. They all flew at the archers, scattering their ranks. By "flew" I'm not speaking metaphorically. Black, leathery wings concealed in their lumpy backs unfolded and spread wide. The demons scattered our archers, falling on them with swords and tridents.

I heard the demons laughing. The sound is much like the calls of a murder of angry crows. I thought my heart might stop and, if it did, I would be grateful.

Some archers survived the attack, but most fell dead. Those who did not die immediately, screamed. The monsters seemed to cherish our anguish and paused, fascinated, before ending the lives of the wounded.

Another red demon appeared from the library's ruins, a sword in his fist. It looked directly at me. I felt like I had telescopic vision. It wasn't possible, I suppose, but in that moment, I could have sworn that, even at that distance, I could see the demon's yellow eyes narrow as he zeroed in on me. He dropped lightly to the ground and began to run my way.

All I had was a *bokken*, but seeing St. Charles die the way he did built my anger higher than my fear could reach. I ran at the red demon. I'm not sure which of us was more surprised.

# 36

I ran as hard as I could. He was huge and covered ground quickly. Had I run from him, he would have taken me down before I got halfway to the ruined church. I would have died screaming, a meal for a demon, within sight of my father's grave.

I was almost out of breath when I came at him, screaming a war cry, bokken raised high. The thing laughed at me and my spine went cold. He raised his sword and cut the air in a wide, horizontal arc as I slid on my knees across the wet grass and leaned way back.

His weapon missed kissing my nose by an inch. Add a few more inches to that and the monster would have hacked my skull in half like a rotten melon. Instead, I rolled up to my feet behind him.

Before my attacker could turn on me, I sprinted for the nearest pad, just to the right. It was the only training pad that might give me some small advantage: the circle of pipes.

The space was narrow in that circular forest. I angled my body in as the demon's roar and his thick blade followed me. He reached in, straining. I thought I was clear of him until, with one savage lunge, he tried to open my throat. The tip of his blade cut my hair short on one side instead.

As the demon leaned in again, trying to end me, I wriggled away. The taser was no longer at my waist and I'd dropped my helmet in the explosion. All I had was the dull wooden practice sword and the thick cloth belt that had held the taser. I pulled off the belt and, when the demon next tried to cut me with his sword, I wrapped his thick wrist with it.

He yanked his hand back and my head rang off one of the steel pipes. But I didn't let go. I wrapped the end of my belt around another pole to gain leverage and hauled on it with all my might. I braced against the steel poles with my legs and used all my weight.

I heard shots nearby. It was Manhattan, running forward and firing, two-handed. Very John Woo. The monster in my trap shuddered and screamed in rage.

I prayed Manny's ammo had been blessed by celibate monks who really were celibate and not faking it. My prayer was answered when I saw the monster's yellow eyes go wide in pain as the holy rounds burned holes through his torso.

Manny arrived and stepped too close as I was tying the belt around a pipe. The demon surged and spread his leathery wings, knocking my rescuer off her feet.

The demon laughed then. I hate the sound of a demon laughing. I picked up my wooden practice sword.

Lesson 74: Even a dull wooden sword can kill if you shove its tip as deep and as hard as you can through a red demon's wide yellow eye. The monster's brain is a small target. Press hard and rotate the sword in circles until you find it. Try not to barf. The insides of every demon smells like rotten Brussel sprouts on top of burning electronics.

My attacker slumped to the ground, one clawed hand still tied to a pipe.

I ran to Manhattan and pulled her up as she was changing mags on her pistols. The demons across the courtyard were finished with the Choir's brave archers and soon they would turn their attention to us.

"I can't pull off that trick twice." I said. "We have to get to heavier weapons."

We ran for our lives. I'd seen that in movies and heard the phrase a few times. It seemed like a silly cliche. When you really have to run for your life, you worry a lot and you're pretty sure it's a race you're about to lose. Your back feels vulnerable. You try to run faster than your top speed.

Lesson 75: You cannot, no matter how scared you are, run faster than your top speed just because you are terrified.

It seemed there was nothing to stop the invaders from reaching the barracks now. Once inside, they would kill all our forces, room by room. Those great wings would knock us off our feet. The tridents would thrust and plunge. Once we were all trapped and crippled, they'd put down their spears and swords. Then they'd use the weapons they were born with. They'd make us into sweetbread pizza by claw and fang.

The demons didn't get the chance. Their wide and clear way was across an open courtyard. It was not to be an easy defeat of the Choir. The open courtyard looked like an invitation to the enemy. Instead, it was a field of fire.

At the sound of the gatling guns, I remembered Victor's words. "This courtyard is a trap," he'd told me. "The Oracle says a great battle will take place here, in these courtyards."

When Victor mentioned his charms and enchantments, I'd pretty much shrugged it off. I'd been impressed with the power of the lamp of Tighloon, but it was at best a tool and at least a curiosity.

And, I confess, when Victor had mentioned he had his very own Oracle, all I could think of was the black woman in *The Matrix* who (spoiler alert!) turned out to be a computer program.

I pressed against a courtyard wall, transfixed by the sight of the demons shot from the air and falling to the ground like clay pigeons. When I craned my neck, I could see Vlad at the gun in the central tower of the West dividing wall. Victor manned a gatling gun in the East tower. The invaders were caught in a crossfire.

I thanked God for the Oracle, or, Whoever Is in Charge, anyway. I love science, but magic is often less longwinded in reaching conclusions and solving problems.

In a few moments, the red invaders were dead. I'd almost forgotten about the blue demons. Gog and Magog flew along the courtyard wall from their station in the library, turned in a tight loop and came up the West dividing wall behind Vlad.

Before he could turn his gun on them or even draw a blade, the pair of demons seized his arms. They threw the man who could not tell a lie to the ground far below.

I heard the crack of Vlad's spine as he hit the concrete. The training pad was a circle of stairs that went nowhere.

In a blink, it looked like Vlad Estasia was dying in the middle of an Escher sketch.

Lesson 76: You don't hate demons enough.

# 37

Victor told me later that, in *Revelation*, Gog and Magog symbolize all future enemies of the Kingdom of God.

I'm not up on my *Bible*. Mama is a red letter Presbyterian. "I just read the words in red to skim what Jesus said. I assume I got the gist."

Interpretations of the *Book of Revelation* are a labyrinth. I've tried to find the way through, but I just get lost. I don't know about Whoever's In Charge. However, as Vlad fell, I believed Gog and Magog were surely *my* enemies. I didn't just swear to kill the blue demons for murdering Vlad. I swore to *obliterate* them. If they liked eating humans so much, I thought, maybe it was time to see what blue demon tastes like.

I didn't get the chance for vengeance. The bright blue demons roared and soared as the Choir's reinforcements arrived. From the Keep, fresh soldiers boiled into the archer's courtyard and rushed to join the fight. They wore the armor of many ages. The Sword Section that had retreated carrying wooden swords returned to the field of battle with guns and swords and crossbows. When I saw them coming, I even believed in angels for a moment.

One of the monsters, I didn't know which was which, flew over the bailey and disappeared from sight. The other retreated behind the West courtyard wall and reappeared only briefly to disappear back into the smoking library. Shots were fired, but too late to kill or even wound the monster.

One went back to his world. The other was loose in ours.

I ran to Vlad. He lay shattered atop the concrete stairs. He still breathed, but barely.

"Don't worry," I said. "We'll get you help."

Through shallow breaths, Vlad said, "I am not worried. I am beyond help." He coughed and a trickle of blood slid from the corner of his mouth. He frowned. "I am a little worried."

Manhattan bent over him, assessing his injuries. When she sat up, she shook her head. I asked her if magic would help him.

"Magic is good for tricks and blessings and charms and an evening with Penn and Teller. Shaman's suck at this sort of thing," she said.

Vlad nodded slightly and it hurt him. "If the shamans were more capable, we wouldn't need oncologists and orthopedic surgeons. Besides, even Maimonides Medical Center is too far away for me now."

I began to cry as the Choir gathered in a huge circle. "What do we do?"

Vlad coughed. "Wait." Then he coughed up more blood. "This will not take long."

Manny slid an open hand under the big man's left fist so he could take it if he wanted to and she wouldn't hurt

234

him.

He clutched it and reached for my hand, as well. His hand was cold. I felt for his pulse. It was weak and slowing.

He smiled at me. "I think I have enough evidence…to answer your earlier question more conclusively…" He began to pant. "I am…not…a robot."

"You saved us all," I said. "You and Victor saved us all."

Vlad's smile disappeared. "Not all."

"We won the battle," I said.

Vlad managed to shake his head. I thought he would say something more, but his stare went on too long and he stopped breathing.

"Call for help!" I said. "Please! There's got to be someth — " but when I touched his chest, I knew there was nothing more to be done. Beneath Vlad's suit jacket, his shirt was soaked blood red and his chest was like a soft bag, every bone shattered. His chest had been opened with the slashes of three sharp claws. The wound was as deep as the trace of long knives.

I searched the faces of the Choir. I did not see Vlad's ghost among the armored throng.

Lesson 77: We all need at least one person in our lives who will tell the truth.

The crowd parted for Victor. He stood over his fallen friend and said, "Just as the Oracle predicted."

I caught Manhattan's eye. She looked furious. "Too bad the Oracle couldn't be more specific about which rainy afternoon the attack would come."

"Wait," I said. "Victor, you told me *you* were supposed to die in an attack in the courtyard."

"In the final attack. This wasn't the final attack. It was only a small force that got through. And they devastated us. This is just the end of the beginning. We have a long war ahead, and that's if we're successful."

Mr. Chang, his face still smeared with blood, appeared beside Victor. I looked from Vlad to Victor to my martial arts teacher. "You guys aren't named after places," I said absently. "What city or town or state will fall without Vlad fighting for it?"

"I started the Choir Invisible," Victor said. "Vlad was the first to join me."

"I was the third," Mr. Chang said. "Peter Smythe was fourth."

I looked away from the dead man at my feet to the fallen bodies of the Choir's defenders.

"It's bad luck that Vlad's name wasn't Russia," Victor said. "With him gone, I don't feel like his home nation is in danger of falling to demons. It feels like the whole Choir is vulnerable."

Tears welled in my eyes and slipped down my cheeks. "We won today's battle at too terrible a cost."

"We lost," Mr. Chang said. "They pushed more forces through the rift than they ever have. They'll do it again. They're getting stronger while our barrier weakens. Our archer section is depleted. One of the blue demons got out into the world."

"The biggest loss is St. Charles," Manhattan said. "With the library destroyed, how can we close the rift? Somewhere in the library's ashes was the secret to how we could close the passages between dimensions."

Victor looked from face to face. I expected him to give one of his rousing, eloquent speeches. I thought he'd motivate and inspire. Instead, the old man said, "Well... shit."

Lesson 78: No use preaching to the Choir.

# 38

New York City is a surprisingly good place for wars with demons. Mayor Bill de Blasio has a secret Magical and Demoniacal PR Department. It's just one public relations guy, but he can keep a secret. His sole purpose is to cover up anything that would divulge the fact that the Secret City swarms with ghosts and is sometimes invaded by demons.

Any strange sights and the noises of warfare are easily explained away. Worried inquiries are answered with cover ups and sometimes a few payoffs.

The magic words are, "We're filming a movie." The addition of, "Mila Kunis will star in it," makes New Yorkers nod knowingly.

That giant, flying blue demon you thought you saw? *Nah.* It was a drone in a Halloween suit that went off course from the movie set, last seen over Jersey.

New York City has forty or so billionaires, a thriving stock exchange and millions of tourists. The PTB don't want to mess with that. They'll keep up the pretense that Armageddon isn't coming. The subways will keep running and you'll still be able to buy tickets to Mets games right up until the moment fire rains down from the sky and legions of horned devils march down Wall Street.

Gee. When the demon hordes do finally break through to our dimension, I hope they at least *start* with Wall Street.

Manny flew back to Iowa with me for one day and a night. I had spoken to Mama not at all and had texted her less and less. It was time to see her again, sit down and hash out the past over one of her barbecue chicken dinners. I'd scream a lot and pout a little and we'd make peace over lemon meringue pie. She'd kept secrets and she did things she shouldn't have, but Mama's heart was where she always left it: in the right place.

Before I went home to see Mama, though, there was something else to do. Manny and I rented an SUV at the Oskaloosa airport and loaded a heavy steamer trunk into the back.

"Don't worry," Manny said. "We'll take care of your BAE."

"Is that short for 'baby?'" I asked.

"Seriously?"

"Yeah. I mean, I assume..."

"Oh, Iowa. As soon as we get back to Brooklyn, we're going shopping and I'll give you a crash course. If you're going to be a New Yorker, you need lessons in how to blend in." She looked me up and down. "With style."

She reached out and squeezed my hand to let me know she wasn't as harsh as she sounded. "BAE. *B-A-E.* Before Anything Else."

"Brad was Before *Everything* Else," I said. "He was my BEE. Now, I don't even know the girl who was Brad's honey. I think she died a little in a mental hospital. Then she died a lot after…after New York."

"As long as you commit to wearing so much plaid flannel and thinking of him as your BEE and you as his honey, you haven't changed that much. Your dead boyfriend will still recognize you."

"Manny?"

"Yeah, hon?"

"*Sh*. It's short for shut up."

"Sorry."

We drove to Medicament and went straight to the Evers farm, back to the tall grasses. In my absence, the tall grasses had lain flat. My dead farm boy boyfriend had not.

Brad stared at us as we got out of the SUV. Winter would hit soon and it was time to set Brad free.

Lesson 79: Every human life is priceless and far too short. It doesn't matter if you die young or old, the tragedy carries just as much weight in tears for those who loved the dead.

I blanked out for a moment and, when I paid attention again, Manny was speaking. "We'll start with new shoes. As fashionistas go, you're a fixer upper."

"As long as the shoes have toe caps. I'm working at the funeral home on Monday."

"What? Why?"

"Sam finally called. She has a shift for me at Castille."

"Still waiting on the why," she said. "It's a funeral home. Funerals are what the Choir Invisible is meant to prevent."

"Because there is more than one way to serve. Because funerals are for the living."

When we pulled up at the Evers farm, the place looked

deserted except for Brad's ghost. He stood not fifty paces from where the baler ripped his arms away.

He stared at me as we stepped out of the SUV. I saw my dead farm boy boyfriend a little differently now. I wasn't blinded by tears and emotions. No iron-winged butterflies beat at my insides. I saw my lover as a young man trapped in a process he did not understand. I didn't understand much more than he did, but now I knew what to do.

"Um...Brad?" I called. "Look at the sky, honey. The clouds are changing every minute. You aren't changing just standing there. It's time to join the natural processes of life, okay? We're going to figure this out so you can move on. It's going to be good, I think."

He stared at me, saying nothing. I tried not to look at the bloody stumps at his shoulders.

Manny opened the back of the truck and, together, we lowered the steam trunk to the soft shoulder of the road. A few minutes later, we wrestled the lamp of Tighloon over the fence.

The lamp glowed and, behind Brad, the echo of his life's only anguish appeared. In bright white and dark black and shades of gray, we saw what happened. Manny and I watched as Brad, still alive, brought the big baling machine to a halt. Dead Brad turned to watch, too.

Live Brad climbed down from the baling machine to speak to a tall man in a fedora and a long coat. We couldn't see his face yet. All I could see was that he had a broad back.

Showing off his deep dimples, Brad smiled broadly as he removed his work gloves to greet the man. He held out his hand to shake.

The tall man seized Brad's hand and threw him toward the whirling teeth of the huge machine. Brad stopped himself before the blades got him, but the big man grabbed him again.

Manny drew in a sharp breath. "Oh, no. No. Oh, no. Oh, my god!"

I looked away as the murder progressed. Dead Brad watched himself, his face darkening as the echo's events unfolded along their bloody course.

When it was done, Brad's black and white echo, now armless, stumbled back toward his family's house.

The big man turned to watch him go and, for a moment, his face came into focus as Brad looked back at him in terror.

Manny took in another deep breath and let it out through her teeth in a slow hiss. "For a minute there, I was almost sure the bad guy would turn out to be Vlad. Same build."

"Yeah. I thought it was a jerk from high school who cut in front of me at a water fountain once," I said. "I wish it was that guy who murdered Brad. That would make more sense. An angry used car salesman with 'roid rage and a history of concussions would make more sense. But you know who that was, right?"

Manny nodded and studied my face. "You recognized him, too."

Tears slipped down my cheeks. "Yes. I know the man who killed Brad."

"I thought you didn't remember him," Manny said.

"From Mama's hidden album. She thinks I don't know where she hides the pictures, but she takes the old pictures out once in a while, when she's drinking. That's Peter

Smythe. From Mama's wedding album. My father."

"It's got to be…I don't know, some kind of enchantment. Peter Smythe is dead. He's buried by the Keep's destroyed church."

"Apparently not."

I turned to my dead farm boy boyfriend for the last time. "I'm so sorry. If he wasn't my father…if I didn't live here…if you didn't live here…if I hadn't asked you to the Halloween dance…if, if, if…"

I hadn't allowed his ghost to get this close before. I reached out and touched Brad's cheek.

I felt his anger and my sadness. I felt loss, his and mine. I thought of his last message to me. After he hung up on the 911 operator screaming at him to stay on the line, he struggled to dial the phone with a pencil in his teeth to leave a message for me.

"I will *never* hold you in my arms again, Tam." That's all he could manage before he fell to the floor.

Until I understood his anger, I thought that message — the utter loss in his voice — carried all the love and passion in the world. Now I saw Brad's message was sent in sadness, but fury, too. When I checked my dents-for-dimples blind spot, I knew I'd misunderstood his last message completely.

Why my father killed Brad, I didn't know with certainty. I guessed he killed Brad to make me a shade seer and a member of the Choir Invisible.

"Tamara?" Manny put a hand on my shoulder. "There's nothing more the lamp can show us unless you want to see it happen again."

"I don't." My gaze stayed on Brad. Instead of receiving his anger, I sent him my memories.

"Remember Christmas night? You and me, naked under the Christmas tree lights? Remember how I took your hand and pulled you out to the tall grass? Remember how we laughed so much?"

Brad's anger softened as his sadness grew deeper.

"It's time to find out what's next," I said. "Wherever you go, forget about me. Whatever happens, I don't think you have to suffer loss anymore. I hope not."

Manny handed me the canteen. She said a prayer as I uncapped it.

Brad shook his head. He leaned close and I trembled. I drank from the canteen in long, deep swallows. I closed my eyes as he leaned forward and kissed my wet lips. For a fleeting second, I thought I felt his arms wrap around me again. It was like our first warm embrace at the Halloween dance. On our first date, I'd been dressed as a fighter in a Hapkido *gi*. Brad was a zombie.

*Circles.*

When I opened my eyes, Brad was gone, off to find out what comes next.

Manny took me in her arms. I cried into her neck. After a long time, she gently kissed my tears away. "It's okay, sister," she said. "It's okay."

"Yeah. Sure. Everything's great." I straightened and looked at the sky. The clouds had set sail under a high wind, moving north. Darkness would fall soon. It was time to go home.

Mama would fix her chicken. We'd eat lemon meringue pie in front of the television.

Tomorrow Manny and I would return to our lives in New York, for however long our lives and New York lasted.

"The demons will come," I told Manny. "That's inevitable, isn't it?"

"Vlad would have agreed," Manny said.

"You knew my father."

"The man I knew was Peter Smythe," she said. "I can't imagine why he would do that to your boyfriend. He was a demon killer."

"I think he did it to make me like him."

Manny stayed quiet so long I thought she would add nothing. Finally, she said, "The demons have their seers, too," Manny said. "It's a sure bet that when war comes, Iowa, Castrator of Demons, is a big player. They know who you are. Maybe Peter did what he did to make you strong. If they showed up here…without singers like you, awake and alive, singing war cries and swinging swords —"

"That wasn't his choice to make," I said. "Victor said my father died in the spring."

"We thought he did," Manny said.

"Obviously, he didn't. No matter what his reasons, he killed Brad. When I find Peter Smythe, I'll kill him."

"You're talking patricide, Tam."

"Killing close relatives isn't just for royal families, Manny. Not when they deserve it. Peter Smythe is definitely weakening the barrier between human snacks and hungry demons."

"But maybe he was trying to strengthen th — "

"His reasons don't matter. His actions matter. If he was trying to make me into a singer for the Choir, he succeeded. But he killed Brad. He killed everything I was going to be."

"Well, yeah," Manhattan said. "That's not cool."

# 39

And now, candidates, we look to the future. I think we'll win because the demons only know hate. We're fighting for peace and love. They're fighting against toddler sandwiches and human pancreas pizza.

The Choir Invisible will scour Twitter for new recruits among the psychics and ghost hunters and paranormal investigators. We'll seek you out in mental hospitals and homeless shelters. Together, we'll fight with ancient weapons for the love of sweet coffee and the joys of living in the 21$^{st}$ century.

Our swords and spears and arrows and blessed ammo will cut and chop and mash. The Choir Invisible will sing. The demons will fall.

We will leave a legacy of safety. We will never allow children's fears of the monsters under the bed to become a reality in this dimension.

Lesson 80: It's hard to let the dead stay dead, of course. In quiet moments, I still think of my farm boy boyfriend. I remember his confidence and his dimples and the way he made me laugh and the way he made me feel when he was mine and I was his.

As I write this, I am preparing for war, focusing on the tasks ahead and living as much and as well as I can, while I can. I am doing, not crying.

Mine is just another of those farm-girl-runs-from-ghosts-and-moves-to-the-big-city-to-slay-demons-and-discovers-her-true-calling-coming-of-age stories. It's a glorious and mean and tragic start. The best stories all start that way. I hope you'll continue on this journey with me so it doesn't end as it began. We have to turn this circle into a straight line that ends in a happier place. That is everyone's job, whether they sing in the Choir or not.

Lesson 81: The pain of losing those we love never really goes away. I still love Brad, but you and I have much to lose and so much more to win.

I cannot rush to follow Brad into whatever comes next. Singers have too much to do and no time to waste. The world doesn't know it, but they depend on us.

Join the Choir Invisible and fight for the living. I have learned that when you fight for life despite everything you have lost, the haunting lessens.

# A NOTE TO THE READERS

Hello, Dear Reader,

True story:

A few days ago, I moved a couple of bodies. I needed the money. It was a horror and that's the truth of capital *D*, Death. The blood and the sores on the tongue…now is not the time to go into what I saw and what I had to do. You don't want to know the details of cold skin through thin, Nitrile gloves, the wild gaze of the deceased and congealed blood stretching between the pale lips of a slack maw. My point is, I've written a lot of dark and gritty stuff, some of it based on real life. *The Haunting Lessons*, my first deep foray into urban fantasy, is more upbeat and fun. I have a couple of people to thank for that.

A young writer approached me for help with her first publication. Holly (Pop) Papandreas had a true story. It was an intriguing and creepy novella and she told her story well. Holly wanted to share it with the world but she wasn't sure how. She worried about reviews and the thousand little details behind publishing any ebook. I encouraged her to write and helped her out with some technical details. You'll find her short story, *Ouija, A True Story*, on Amazon.

We talked and talked some more and pretty soon I had our main character, Tam, based on my new friend. We traded story beat ideas back and forth and pretty soon we had a couple of collaborations going. Our first story outline was about hunting demons in New York. It was fun, but a bit short for a novel. I put it aside for a future project. The future showed up on my doorstep sooner than expected. The future is like that.

About the same time, Jerry Benns, publisher of Charon Coin Press, approached me with an idea I didn't really care for. He asked if I wanted to contribute to an anthology. Jerry's a nice guy and I loved the idea of being part of another anthology. (I'd been part of the *Horror Within Box Set* and I will soon contribute to a non-fiction anthology with my friend Sher Kruse, the author of *Butterfly Stitching*.)

Good news, except Jerry wanted a ghost story for his anthology. I'd never really written a ghost story and wasn't into it. I put Jerry off and told him I'd noodle with the idea. As often happens, I awoke with insomnia (again) and, in the fleeting, hypnagogic state between waking and dreaming, ghosts and demons came together in one, larger story. I called Holly and the project got moved up in my schedule.

It would have been easier to give Jerry the first few chapters of this book and stop at, "Psychiatry works!" (I love that line.) That would have been fine. But tears and stories do find their way, don't they?

Our outline awaited and I pounded out the first draft of

*The Haunting Lessons* in eighteen days during National Novel Writing Month. This is my sixteenth book, but it wouldn't have been so light and fun without Holly's input, so she's co-author.

I still owe Jerry a ghost story for his anthology. I'll give him one. The muse is never further away than another terrible bout of insomnia. Jerry also has my thanks for spurring me to write in a genre I did not initially groove on. I found my groove outside of my comfort zone, much as Tam did in *The Haunting Lessons*. At our best, there's a little Tamara Smythe in all of us. I hope that's true, anyway.

I'm sure you'll see more of Tamara's evolving story in 2015, in books two and three of the *Ghosts and Demons Series*. Holly and I have planned at least three. Three is a power number.

Thank you for reading *The Haunting Lessons*. If you liked this one, please leave a review wherever you bought this book. For a slightly more serious apocalypse, you may enjoy *This Plague of Days*, too. For more on all my books and podcasts, please visit the information hub of my network, **AllThatChazz.com.**

**To find out when the next book in this series is released, sign up for the update letter on the author page at that site.**

Cheers, mates!

~ RCC
December, 2014

# ABOUT THE AUTHORS

**Thanks again for reading**
*The Haunting Lessons,*
*Book One*
**by**
**Holly Pop &**
**Robert Chazz Chute.**

**To find out when the next book in the *Ghosts &***
***Demons Series* will be released,**
**please sign up for the All That Chazz update**
**letter at**
**AllThatChazz.com.**

Holly (Pop) Papandreas is a writer and student. She has
lived in Texas, the Midwest and New York. Her fondest
wish is to write for a living. Be sure to read Holly's creepy
and scary novella,
***Ouija: Based on a True Story.***
\* \* \*

Robert Chazz Chute is a former newspaper and magazine journalist. His writing has won seven awards. He lives in Other London. You can find his blogs, podcasts and many novels at **AllThatChazz.com.**

www.ingramcontent.com/pod-product-compliance
Lightning Source LLC
Chambersburg PA
CBHW030108260626
47156CB00008B/2578